BABY ON BOARD

From bump to baby and beyond…

Whether she's expecting or they're adopting—
a special arrival is on its way!

Follow the tears and triumphs
as these couples find their lives
blessed with the magic of parenthood….

Lex was left nervously eyeing the baby on the floor. Freya sat on her bottom for a while, looking around with wide-eyed interest, then to his alarm she crawled under the table.

Now what? He sat dead still, afraid to move his feet, but after a moment he bent his head very carefully to look under the table and see what she was doing.

Freya's expression was intent as she patted his left shoe, apparently pleased by its shininess. Then the small hands discovered the lace, and pulled at it experimentally. Delighted to find that it came apart if she tugged at it, she looked up to find Lex watching her under the table, and she offered him a gummy smile.

The smile had an odd effect on Lex, and he jerked upright once more and snapped his computer open. Where was Romy? He was terrified to move his feet, but if he was stuck here, he could at least try to get some work done.

"Where's Freya?" Romy asked when she came back at last. For answer, Lex grimaced and pointed wordlessly under the table, and Romy peered beneath to see that her daughter was sucking one of his shoelaces with a thoughtful expression.

JESSICA HART
Juggling Briefcase & Baby

TORONTO • NEW YORK • LONDON
AMSTERDAM • PARIS • SYDNEY • HAMBURG
STOCKHOLM • ATHENS • TOKYO • MILAN • MADRID
PRAGUE • WARSAW • BUDAPEST • AUCKLAND

Recycling programs
for this product may
not exist in your area.

ISBN-13: 978-0-373-74058-1

JUGGLING BRIEFCASE & BABY

First North American Publication 2010

CHAPTER ONE

LEX drummed his fingers on the table and tried to tell himself that the uneasy churning in his gut was due to one too many cups of coffee that morning. He was Alexander Gibson, Chief Executive of Gibson & Grieve, one of the most popular and prestigious supermarket chains in the country, and a man renowned for his cool detachment.

A man like him didn't get *nervous*.

He *wasn't* nervous, Lex insisted to himself. He had been sitting on this damned plane for over an hour now, and if he had to commit himself to flying at thirty thousand feet in little more than a tin can he'd just as soon get it over with, that was all.

See, he wasn't nervous, he was *impatient*.

Lex scowled at the sleety rain streaking the cabin windows, and then stiffened as he caught sight of a limousine speeding across the tarmac towards the plane. His drumming fingers stilled and the churning that wasn't nerves jerked his entrails into a knot so tight that it was suddenly hard to breathe.

She was here.

Very carefully, Lex flexed his fingers and set them flat on the table in front of him while he steadied his breathing.

He wasn't nervous.

Lex Gibson was never nervous.

It was just that the steel band that had been locked around his chest for the past twelve years had been steadily tightening ever since he had heard that Romy was back in the country.

It had notched tighter when Phin had casually announced that he had offered her a job in Acquisitions.

And tighter still when Tim Banks, Director of Acquisitions, had rung that morning to explain that a family crisis meant that he would have to miss accompanying Lex on the most important deal of his life.

'But I've arranged for Romy Morrison to go with you instead,' Tim had said. 'She's been working with me on the negotiations, and has built up an excellent rapport with Willie Grant himself. I know how important this meeting is, Lex, and I wouldn't suggest her unless I was sure she was the best. I've sent a car to pick her up, and she'll be with you as soon as possible.'

And now here she was, and the steel band was clamped so painfully around his lungs that it hurt to breathe. Lex forced his attention back to the email he had been reading, but the screen kept blurring in front of his eyes. It would be fine. Romy was an employee, nothing more.

He wanted this deal with Grant more than he had ever wanted anything else and if Romy could help him persuade Grant to sign, that was all that mattered. The sooner she got on this plane, the sooner they could get the deal done.

He was *impatient*. That was all.

The car had barely stopped by the steps of the executive jet before Phil, the driver, was out and holding open the door for Romy.

'Mr Gibson doesn't like to be kept waiting,' he had said anxiously, watching Romy run around the flat, frantically ticking off items on a mental list.

'Nappies…travelling cot…high chair…oh, God, the *car seat*! Yes, I *know* he's been waiting an hour already…I'm coming, I'm coming…'

Travelling with Freya was nerve-racking at the best of times, and Romy had been so flustered by the thought of coming face to face with Lex again that she had forgotten first the pushchair and then the changing mat, until Phil, forced to turn round and drive back to the flat twice, was beside himself.

He was clearly terrified of Lex. Almost everyone who worked for Gibson & Grieve found their chief executive intimidating, to say the least.

Romy wasn't terrified, or even intimidated. But she was very nervous about coming face to face with him all the same. Sitting alone in the back of the limousine as they crawled through the rush-hour traffic, she had swung wildly between wondering what else she had left behind, and wondering what she would say when she saw Lex again.

What she would *feel*.

Best not to feel anything, Romy had decided. Lex clearly wanted nothing to do with her. He had made no effort to talk to her at Phin's wedding, and not once in the six months she had been working for Gibson & Grieve had he found an excuse to speak to her.

Perhaps she could have found an excuse to talk to *him*, Romy acknowledged, but what could she have said?

I've never forgotten you.

Sometimes I think about your mouth, and it feels as if you've laid a warm hand on my back, making me clench and shiver.

Have you ever thought about me?

No, she definitely couldn't have asked *that*.

It was all so long ago now. Twelve years ago. Romy looked out of the window and sighed. She was thirty now, and a mother, and Lex was her boss, not her lover. You didn't worry about how you felt about your boss. You just did your job.

So that was what she would do.

Romy glanced doubtfully down at her daughter. It wasn't going to be easy to be coolly professional with Freya in tow, but she would manage it.

Somehow.

Phil already had the boot open and was starting to unload all Freya's stuff, while the pilot, spotting their arrival, set the engines whining impatiently. The message was clear: Alexander Gibson was waiting to go.

Cravenly, Romy wished she could stay in the car, but then she remembered the desperation in Tim's voice.

'*Please*, Romy,' he had begged. 'Sam needs me, but Lex has got to have someone from the team with him when he meets Grant, too. If we let him down on this one, I don't know what he'll do, but it won't be pleasant.'

No one else would do, Tim had said, and in the end Romy had given in. She owed Tim too much to let him down when he needed her most. So she scrambled awkwardly out of the car, Freya in one arm and her laptop in the other, and, putting her head down against the rain, she ran up the steps to the plane.

A flight attendant wearing a badge that read 'Nicola' was waiting to greet her at the cabin door, and, in the face of her perfectly groomed appearance, Romy found herself hesitating. It had been such a rush to get ready that she hadn't had time to wash her hair, put on any make-up, or do more than throw on some clothes, and now she was going to have to face Lex looking a complete mess.

Too bad, she told herself, lifting her chin. He was lucky she was here at all.

Taking a deep breath, she smiled in response to Nicola's greeting, hoisted Freya higher on her hip and ducked into the cabin.

The plane was narrow but luxuriously fitted-out. It had squashy leather seats, a plush carpet, glossy wooden trim everywhere. But Romy didn't notice any of it.

Lex sat, halfway down the cabin, a laptop open on the table in front of him, looking up over his glasses, and as their eyes met it seemed to Romy that everything stilled. Behind her, Phil and Nicola had paused, while the sounds of the airport faded abruptly, until the whine of the engines, the rumble and scream of planes taking off and landing, the crackle of the radio as the pilot checked in with the control tower, were all strangely muted and there was only the warm weight of Freya in her arms and the man whose pale grey eyes set her heart thudding painfully in her throat.

'Hello, Lex,' she managed, hoping that he would blame her dash up the steps for the breathless note in her voice.

'Romy.'

Lex didn't even see the baby at first. His first reaction was one of relief, so sharp it was almost painful. She wasn't as beautiful as he'd remembered. Oh, it was unmistakably Romy, with that tumble of dark hair and those huge dark eyes, but the enchanting, passionate girl he'd fallen so disastrously in love with had gone. The years had blurred the pure lines of her face and faded the once gorgeous bloom of youth and she was just a dishevelled young woman with a tired face and a baby in her arms.

Thank God, thought Lex, feeling the band around his heart ease very slightly.

There was a beat, and then his mind caught up with his eyes, in a double take so startled that it would have been comical if Lex had felt anything like laughing, which he didn't.

With a *what* in her arms? A *baby*?

Romy's baby. Another man's baby. The steel band contracted once more.

His brows snapped together. 'What,' he demanded, 'is that baby doing here?'

'This is Freya.' Romy put up her chin at his tone. Was that really all he had to say, after twelve years?

She was furious. With Lex, for daring to sit there, looking like that. Looking as if he had never kissed her, as if he had never made her senses snarl with the touch of his hand. As if he had never loved her.

With herself, for being so bitterly disappointed.

What had she expected, after all? That he would sweep her back into his arms? That the heat would still crackle between them, after twelve long years?

Fool.

'I explained to Tim that I would have to bring her with me,' she said in a voice quite as cold as Lex's. She could do remote and chilly just as well as he could. 'Didn't he tell you?'

'What?'

'Tim said he would clear it with Willie Grant's people.'

Lex wasn't listening. Behind Romy, he could see the driver unloading pushchairs and carry cots and God only knew what else into the cabin. 'What the hell is going on? You,' he snapped at Phil, who froze guiltily. 'Take all that stuff off right now!'

'Yes, sir.'

'Just a minute,' said Romy clearly, advancing down the cabin towards Lex. 'Freya needs all that.'

Lex snatched off his glasses. 'For God's sake, Romy, you're not seriously proposing to bring a *baby* along on a business trip?'

'I don't have a choice. I told Tim all this, and he assured me that it wouldn't be a problem.'

'No problem?' he echoed in disbelief. 'We're on the verge of negotiating a major deal with a difficult client and you don't think it's a problem to turn up with a baby in tow? We'll look totally unprofessional! It's out of the question,' he said with finality.

Romy was strongly tempted to turn on her heel and walk out, but if she did that, what would happen to Tim, and the deal the whole team had worked so hard on?

Drawing a breath, she struggled to keep her temper under control. 'I was under the impression that you wanted someone from Acquisitions to ac-company you?'

'I do want you,' said Lex, and for one horrible moment the words seemed to jangle in the air, a bitter parody of the ones he had once murmured against her skin.

I love you. I want you. I need you.

He folded the glasses he wore when working at a computer and put them in the breast pocket of his shirt. 'I just don't want a baby.'

'Well, I'm sorry,' said Romy, 'but you can't

have me without her. What do you want me to do, leave her on the tarmac?'

Lex scowled. 'Haven't you got…I don't know…childcare or something? What do you do when you're at work? Or is Acquisitions doubling as a nursery these days?'

Romy set her teeth at the sardonic note in his voice. 'She goes to the crèche at the office.'

'There's a crèche?'

'Yes, there's a crèche,' she said, holding onto her temper with difficulty.

'One of Phin's projects, I suppose.' Lex looked disapproving. His brother had reluctantly joined the company after their father's stroke, and Lex had put him in charge of staff development. It was meant to be a token position, but he was always coming across initiatives in unlikely places nowadays.

'I believe so,' said Romy in a cool voice. 'It's one of the reasons Gibson & Grieve is such a popular place to work.'

'Well, then, why can't the baby go there?'

'Because we're going to be away overnight, and the crèche closes at six. I don't know anyone else I can leave her with, especially not at this short notice. Tim only rang a couple of hours ago. I *explained* all this.'

Freya was getting heavy, and Romy shifted her to the other hip as she glared at Lex in frustration.

Part of her was almost glad to find Lex so unreasonable. It made it easier to pretend that he was just a difficult boss.

Easier to forget how warm his hands had been, how sure his lips. How a rare smile would illuminate that austere face and warm the cool grey eyes.

'I don't think you quite realise how difficult it has been for me to get here this morning,' she went on crisply. 'I'm here because Tim seemed to think that it was important, but if you'd rather go on your own, that's fine by me.'

A muscle was working in Lex's cheek. 'It *is* important. I need someone who's up to speed on the details of the acquisition.'

'Then perhaps you would prefer to rearrange?' she suggested, and Lex made an irritable gesture.

'No, we're going today. I understand from Tim that Grant's not that keen on the deal, and it's taken long enough to get him to see me. If we start messing around and changing dates, it could jeopardise the whole deal and I don't want to do that. We've been working on this too long to throw it away now.'

Romy said nothing.

Lex glared at her. There was only one choice, and they both knew it.

'Oh, for God's sake, bring all that stuff back,' he snapped at Phil, who exchanged a look with Nicola and went back down the steps into the rain to collect everything that he'd just stashed back in the boot of the car. 'Tell the pilot we're ready to go as soon as you're clear. We've wasted enough time this morning.'

Annoyed, he smacked the lid of his computer down and directed another irritable look at Romy. 'You'd better sit down,' he said, pointing at the seat opposite him. '*And* the baby.'

'Freya,' said Romy, not moving.

'What?'

'Her name's Freya.'

Her chin was up, and the dark eyes looked directly back into his.

And Lex felt the world shift around him, just as it had done all those years ago. She was closer now, close enough for him to see the fine lines starring her eyes, and he struggled to hold onto his conviction that she was just tired and untidy and nothing special.

But his gaze kept catching on the lovely curve of her mouth, and when he looked back at her he had the horribly familiar sensation of falling into those eyes. Lex had never understood how so rich and dark a brown could be so luminous. He wasn't a fanciful man, but it had always seemed to him as if light glowed in their depths, warming and beckoning.

How could he have thought for a moment that she wasn't as beautiful as ever?

Twelve years ago, he had fallen into those eyes, heedless of the consequences. He had lowered his guard and made himself vulnerable, and there was no way he was going through that again.

Lex willed himself not to look away, but he had himself back under control. He could do this. All he had to do was think about the deal. That was all that mattered now, and the fact was that he needed Romy. Without Tim Banks, she was his connection to Willie Grant, and he wouldn't put it past her to take the wretched baby and walk off the plane. She always had been stubborn.

'Very well,' he said tightly. 'You *and Freya* had better sit down.'

'Thank you,' said Romy, and sat down opposite him, calmly buckling her seat belt and settling the baby—*Freya*—on her lap.

Lex's jaw worked as he regarded her with a kind of baffled resentment. She was mighty cool considering that he was Chief Executive and she was just a temporary employee, and a far from senior one at that.

This was all Phin's fault.

Twelve years. That was how long he had spent trying to forget Romy, and the moment he laid eyes on her again he knew he had been wasting his time. He'd known she was back in the country. He'd known she had a baby. His mother had heard

it from Romy's mother and had sucked in her
breath disapprovingly at the thought of her god-
daughter as a single mother.

'Well, that'll bring Romy home,' she had said.
And it had.

He had even known Romy would be at Phin's
wedding. He'd thought he had braced himself to
meet her again, but when the organ had struck up
and he had turned with Phin to watch Summer
walking up the aisle, all he had seen was Romy,
sitting several rows behind, and his heart had
crumpled at the sight of her. Romy, with her dark,
beautiful eyes and the mouth that had haunted his
memory for so many years. Romy, who had loved
another man and had a baby to show for it.

Lex had avoided her at the reception, and
despised himself for it. He was Chief Executive of
the fastest-growing supermarket chain in England
and Wales. He didn't care about anything but the
success of Gibson & Grieve. He had no trouble
finding a woman if he wanted one. So he should
have been able to greet Romy casually and show her
that he realised her decision had been the right one.

Because of course it was. She had been far too
young to marry. He was eight years older than
her, much too serious to manage all that passion
and spirit. He would have crushed her, or she
would have crushed him, and left him anyway.

The only sensible part of the whole affair was their pact to tell no one else.

So there should have been no problem about meeting her again. But every time he told himself he would go over and say hello there had been someone with her and she had been laughing and waving her arms around so that the collection of bangles she always wore chinked against each other. Or she had been lifting her hand to push the hair away from her neck and he had been gripped by the memory of how soft and silky it had felt twined around his fingers.

And with that memory had come a flood of others that he had failed to forget: the scent of her skin, the husky laugh, the curve of her shoulder and pulse that beat in the base of her throat. That stubborn tilt of her jaw. That smile, the way she had pulled him down to her and made the world go away.

And then Phin was there, clapping him on the shoulder, telling him, almost as an aside, that he had offered Romy a job in Acquisitions.

'What? *Why?*'

'Because she needs a job,' his brother told him. 'She's got a baby to support, and she's having trouble finding work. She's been working overseas and it's hard to get a job when you've got a CV that's quite as varied as hers.'

Lex managed to part his lips and form a

sentence. 'She should have thought about that before she drifted around the world.'

'You put me in charge of staff development,' Phin reminded him unfairly. 'I think Gibson & Grieve needs people with Romy's kind of experience. She was telling me about a diving centre she's been running in Indonesia: she's got all sorts of skills that we can use.'

'Phin, are you sure this is a good idea?'

'Look, it's just a temporary job, replacing Tim Banks's assistant while she's on maternity leave. I think Romy will be good at it, and it'll give her the experience she needs to find a permanent job. It's a win-win situation.'

Lex hadn't been able to object any further, or Phin would have wondered why he was so reluctant to have Romy working for Gibson & Grieve. His brother might seem the most easy-going of men, but Lex was discovering that he was far more perceptive than he seemed.

'Fine,' he had said with shrug, as if he didn't care one way or the other. 'It's your call.'

But Phin wasn't the one who braced himself every day in case he saw her. Who looked up every time the door opened in case it was her. Who had to walk around with a fist squeezed around his heart, just knowing that she was near.

Everything had felt tight for six months now.

His head, his eyes, his heart, his chest. Usually, work was a refuge, but not now, not when Romy could appear at any moment.

So he had seized on the chance of two days away in the Highlands, finalising the deal that would garner Gibson & Grieve a foothold in Scotland at long last. It was something his father had long tried to set up, and Lex, who had spent his life trying to prove that he could run Gibson & Grieve even better than his father, was determined to seal this one and take the company in a new direction that was all his own.

Lex had planned it to be just him and Tim. No entourage, no fuss. Willie Grant, of Grant's Supersavers, was by all accounts a recluse and an eccentric. The last thing Lex wanted was to alienate him by arriving with a lot of unnecessary people. Tim had warned him that Willie was a straight talker, and he wanted to do this face to face. Lex was fine with that. He was a straight talker too.

But now Romy was sitting opposite him instead. With her baby.

At the front of the cabin, Nicola was hurriedly stowing away the extraordinary amount of equipment Romy had seen fit to bring with her. The door had closed after the driver, who had escaped gratefully down the steps, and the pilot was already taxiing, anxious to make up for lost time.

Lex wrenched his mind back from the past and looked at his watch. Two and a half hours behind schedule, and they still had a fair drive after they got to Inverness. Willie Grant lived in a castle in the wilds of Sutherland, in the far north west of Scotland, and God only knew how long it would take to get there. Summer, his PA, would ring and explain the delay, but Lex hated being late.

He hated it when events were out of his control, like this morning. The way they always seemed to be whenever Romy was around.

His life was spent keeping a close guard on himself and his surroundings. Only once had he let it drop, in Paris twelve years ago, when he had lost his head and begged Romy to marry him. Lex had never made that mistake again.

The plane was turning at the end of the runway, and the engines revved until they were screaming with frustration. Then the pilot set them hurtling down the runway.

Lex resisted the temptation to close his eyes and grip the seat arms. He knew his fear was irrational, but he hated being dependent on a pilot. It wasn't the speed that bothered him, or even the thought of crashing. It was putting himself completely in someone else's control.

Romy loved take-off. He remembered how her eyes had shone as the seats pushed into their backs and the power and the speed lifted the plane into the air. Lex hadn't said anything, but she had taken his hand and held it all the way to Paris.

Did she remember?

Lex's face was set with the effort of keeping his gaze on the window, but it was as if his eyes had a will of their own. Like a compass needle being dragged to true north, they kept turning to Romy in spite of the stern message his brain was sending.

The baby, he saw, was looking as doubtful about the whole business as he felt. When the plane lifted off the tarmac and Lex's stomach dropped, she opened her mouth to wail, but Romy bounced her on her lap, distracting her from the pressure in her ears until she was gurgling with laughter.

'You're a born traveller,' Romy told her. 'Just like your old mum.'

She smiled at her daughter and Lex could see the crooked tooth that was so typical of the way Romy just missed being perfect. It was only a tiny kink, only just noticeable, but the faint quirkiness of it gave her face character. He had always thought it made her more beautiful.

Then her eyes met Lex's over the baby's head, and the smile faded.

She was remembering that flight to Paris, too. He could see it in her eyes. The memory was so vivid that they might as well have been back on that plane, side by side, shoulders touching, their hands entwined, her perfume filling his senses as she leaned into him, distracting him with her smile, until it had felt to Lex as if he had left his real self behind and was soaring up with the plane into a different reality where he was a man who didn't care about control or responsibility or being sensible, and could open himself to every pleasure that came his way.

And look where that had got him.

Obviously he might as well have spared himself the effort of looking unconcerned, though. Romy didn't quite roll her eyes at his clenched jaw, but she might as well have done.

'Why didn't you take the train?' she asked.

'It's too far,' said Lex shortly. He hated her thinking that he might be afraid. He wasn't *afraid*, and if he was, he would never admit it.

'It's going to take most of the day to get there as it is. I can't afford to waste all that time sitting on a train. There's too much else to do. I was hoping Grant would be prepared to come to London to discuss the deal.'

Romy shook her head. 'Willie never leaves Duncardie now,' she said. 'His wife died five years ago, and since then he's been a virtual recluse.'

'So Tim explained. He told me that if I wanted

to persuade Willie Grant to agree to the sale, I would have to go there myself.'

'You must want it badly if you're prepared to fly,' said Romy with a faint smile.

'I do.' Lex's face was set in grim lines. 'My father never managed to get a foothold in Scotland, and it was his one big disappointment. If he hadn't had his stroke last year, he'd still be on this plane now, on his way to see Willie Grant. He would never have trusted the negotiations to me.'

'He must have trusted you,' Romy protested. 'You're the one who's carrying on his legacy.'

'Yes, that's what I've been doing,' he agreed, a trace of bitterness in his voice. 'And now I'm ready to move the company in new directions. It's not about my father any more.'

For years he had been trying to prove himself to his father, and now, at last, he had a chance to show him just what he could do with the company.

'This is my deal,' he said. 'The one I made, the one he never could.'

'It's not a competition,' said Romy, but he looked back at her, unsmiling.

'Yes,' he said. 'It is. And it's one I'm going to win. That's why I really needed Tim with me today. If this deal doesn't go through because of his *family crisis*…'

Romy leant forward at that and fixed him with

a look. 'I know you won't take it out on Tim,' she said crisply. 'You're a lot of things, Lex, but you're never unfair, and that would be. Tim has to be with his son. His family has to come first. You know that.'

Lex did know that, but he didn't have to like it. 'I sometimes think it would be easier if we only employed people without families,' he grumbled.

'You wouldn't have a very large workforce in that case.'

'Without children, then. You can be sure that the moment an important deal comes up, the vital person has to go home because some child is ill or needs to be picked up from school or has to be taken to the dentist, and then everybody else has to run around rearranging things to cover for them, like you and Tim.'

'I don't mind,' said Romy, not entirely truthfully. 'I know Tim would do the same for me. It's part of working in a good team.'

Lex grunted. Phin was always going on about teams, but he liked to work on his own. 'That's all very well, but if we're going to make this work I need to know that you're as committed to the success of this deal as Tim is.'

She met his eyes squarely as she settled Freya more comfortably on her lap. 'I am,' she said. 'I owe Tim a lot, and I don't want to let him down.

I owe Gibson & Grieve a lot, too. I know Phin took a risk giving me the job, and I want to prove that I'm worth it. I'll do whatever it takes.'

'Except leave your baby behind,' Lex commented sourly.

'Except that,' she agreed.

CHAPTER TWO

'ACTUALLY, I think Freya could work to our advantage,' Romy said, stroking her daughter's head so that the beaten silver bracelets chittered softly together.

The baby was a funny-looking little thing, Lex thought. She had very fine dark hair that stuck up in an absurd quiff, and round, astounded eyes as dark as her mother's.

'How do you work that out?' he asked, wishing Freya wouldn't stare at him like that. It was disconcerting having that uncompromising gaze fixed so directly on his face.

'Willie Grant is very family-orientated, in spite of the fact that he doesn't have any children of his own. Grant's Supersavers have always been targeted at the family market. It's a big thing with him. To be honest,' Romy said to Lex, 'you're likely to be more of a problem than Freya.'

'*Me?*'

'Willie lives in a very remote place, but he's not isolated. He reads the papers and uses the Internet, and you,' she said, pointing across the table, 'have a reputation.'

'Meaning what?' asked Lex dangerously, and Romy swallowed, remembering, rather too late, that he was her boss. But if they were to secure this deal that meant so much to him, he would have to understand Willie Grant's position.

'Meaning that you've got an image as a loner, unsentimental, a workaholic, none of which makes you seem exactly family friendly.'

Lex narrowed his pale grey gaze. 'So what are you saying, Romy?'

'Just that it would be a mistake to underestimate how strongly Willie feels about family,' she said. 'We had to work very hard to get him to agree to meet you at all. He thinks that you're more interested in profits than in families.'

'Of course I am,' he said with an abrasive look. 'I'm a businessman. Being interested in profits is what I do. My shareholders are more interested in profits too. That doesn't mean we don't offer a service to families. God, we've got children's parking spaces and special trolleys and even crèches in some of the bigger stores, I'm told—what more does Grant want?'

'He wants to feel that he's selling his company

to one with the same ethos,' said Romy evenly. 'We've sold you to Willie on the grounds of your integrity. He'd rather you were a family man but that doesn't mean he doesn't respect your straightforwardness. On the other hand, if you make it obvious that you've got no time for policies that make it easy for your staff to work effectively *and* be effective family members, then I don't think Willie will want to work with you.

'We're not the only retail chain with an interest in Grant's Supersavers,' she told Lex, who scowled. 'He's already had the big four supermarkets up here sniffing around, but he likes Gibson & Grieve's reputation for quality, and he likes the fact that it still has a family connection with you and Phin. But if he doesn't like your attitude,' Romy warned, 'he'll sell to someone else. If you want this deal, Lex, you're going to have to keep on Willie's good side.'

Lex thought about what she had said as he looked out of the window. The plane had burst through the thick cloud layer into dazzling light, but Lex's mind was less on the blueness of the sky up there than on Romy's crisp analysis of his position.

He was more impressed by her than he had expected, he acknowledged to himself. He remembered Romy as a lovely, eager girl, passionate about everything. When she'd talked, she had leant forward with her face alight and her hands moving, encompassing him in her warmth. Now, she was cool and capable, and, in spite of those exotic, distracting bracelets and the distinctly distracting baby, she seemed surprisingly business-like. Lex suspected that Tim would never have dared talk to him so directly, but if Romy was right, then he had needed to hear it.

Because this was all about the deal, and nothing about feelings, right?

Right.

'All right.' He turned back to Romy with a nod of acknowledgement. 'If that's what I have to do to get him to sign, that's what I'll do.'

Romy's expression relaxed. 'It shouldn't be too hard. Just don't tell him you tried to throw Freya off the plane!' She tweaked Freya's nose as she grinned down at her, and the baby chuckled.

Still smiling, Romy glanced up to find Lex watching her, and their eyes snagged for one jarring moment before he looked away.

At the front of the plane, Nicola was making coffee. The smell wafted down the cabin, reminding Romy that she hadn't had time to do more than gulp at a mug of tea that morning.

She unbuckled her seat belt.

'Would you excuse me?' she said formally. 'I didn't even have time to brush my hair this morning, and I'd like to tidy myself up. I presume there's a bathroom of some kind?'

'At the back,' said Lex, then watched in consternation as Romy set Freya on the floor and gathered up her bag. 'Are you just going to leave her there?'

'She can't go anywhere.'

'Well, no, but…shouldn't she be strapped in, or something?'

'Strapped in to what? She's safer on the floor than on a seat she can fall off—unless you'd like to have her on your lap?'

Lex recoiled. 'No!'

'She'll be fine,' Romy soothed. 'I won't be long.'

Romy loved flying. She loved the way her body pressed back into the seat as the plane left the ground. She loved landing and walking across the tarmac with the aircraft fumes shimmering in the heat. She loved looking down onto a billowy carpet of clouds and knowing that she had left everyday life behind and was on her way to somewhere new and exciting.

The only thing she didn't love about flying was using the bathroom. She was used to queuing along the aisle, getting in the flight attendants' way, and manoeuvring awkwardly into narrow cubicles. Being on an executive jet was a whole new experience. Quite apart from the lack of queues, the bathroom here was almost as large as the one in her flat, and sumptuously decorated, with a mirror above a gleaming vanity unit.

Sadly, no amount of flattering lighting could disguise the fact that she looked awful. Romy regarded her reflection with dismay. Her hair was all over the place, there were dark circles under her eyes, and a stain on her blouse marked where Freya had gugged up her hurried breakfast that morning.

Romy rubbed at it with a damp towel, which only seemed to make it worse, so she abandoned that and washed her face instead. Brushing out her hair, she clipped it up in a careless twist and pulled out her make-up bag. By the time she had made up her eyes and put on some lipstick, she was feeling a lot better.

It was going to be OK, she assured her reflection as she brushed down her loose trousers and straightened her top. Now that they had got over the inevitable awkwardness of seeing each other again, everything should be fine.

Of course it was a little strange. Lex was remote, severe, the way he always seemed at work. Looking at him, sitting there in his immaculate suit and tie, you would never guess that he was a man capable of passion, but Romy knew. Whenever she looked at his mouth, or his

hands, she remembered that week in Paris. She remembered how sure his lips had been, how his
touch had made her strum with excitement, how
skilfully he had drawn her into a swirl of heat and
pleasure. She had only been eighteen. How could
she have known that there would never be anyone
else who made her feel quite like that again?

The memory of that week curled voluptu-
ously around the base of Romy's spine and
made her shiver.

'Stop it,' she told herself out loud. 'Stop
thinking about it.'

She had to put that week from her mind. It was
over. Long over. There were more important
things to think about. Freya was her priority now.
Romy had been getting desperate before Phin
offered her this job at Gibson & Grieve, and she
couldn't afford to make a mess of it.

It was only maternity cover, and Jo, whom she
was replacing, would be returning to work soon.
At that point, Romy was going to need a good reference. If she could help Lex close this deal, it
would be fantastic experience for her when it
came to finding another job. A job she needed if
she was to maintain her independence.

That was what she should be thinking about,
not Lex's mouth and how it had once felt on hers.

Romy squared her shoulders. She could do this.

Meanwhile, Lex was left nervously eyeing the baby on the floor. Freya sat on her bottom for a while, looking around with wide-eyed interest, then to his alarm she crawled under the table.

Now what? He sat dead still, afraid to move his feet, but after a moment he bent his head very carefully to look under the table and see what she was doing.

Freya's expression was intent as she patted his left shoe, apparently pleased by its shininess. Then the small hands discovered the lace, and pulled at it experimentally. Delighted to find that it came apart if she tugged at it, she looked up to find Lex watching her under the table, and she offered him a gummy smile.

The smile had an odd effect on Lex, and he jerked upright once more and snapped his computer open. Where was Romy? He was terrified to move his feet in case he kicked the baby by mistake, but if he was stuck here he could at least try and get some work done. He would pretend everything was normal and that there was no baby undoing his shoelaces under the table.

'Where's Freya?' Romy asked when she came back at last.

For answer, Lex grimaced and pointed wordlessly under the table, and Romy peered beneath to see that her daughter had undone both his shoes, and was sucking one of the laces with a thoughtful expression.

'I thought it was an unexploded bomb at least!' she said as she scooped Freya up and straightened.

'I would have been just as nervous,' said Lex grouchily. 'You were gone ages. What have you been doing?'

'I didn't even have time to brush my hair this morning,' Romy pointed out, settling back into her seat. 'I was still in bed when Tim rang. I had a real panic to get here, and I'm still worried I left something vital behind.'

'How could you have left anything behind? It looked as if you brought the entire contents of the house with you!'

She sighed. 'You should see what I left behind! It's not easy to travel light with a baby.'

'You've changed.'

It was a careless comment, but suddenly the air was fraught with memories. There had been a time when Romy would have packed everything she owned into a rucksack.

'Yes,' she said, trying to make her voice as firm and businesslike as possible. 'Yes, I have.' She eyed Lex under her lashes. 'And you?'

'Me?'

'Have you changed?'

He looked away. 'Of course. I'd hope we were both older and a lot wiser.'

Much too wise to run off to Paris for a wild affair, anyway. The unspoken thought hung in the silence that pooled between them until Nicola appeared to offer coffee and biscuits.

'Thank you.' Romy was grateful for the interruption, but even more for the sustenance. She hadn't had time for breakfast that morning.

Freya's eyes lit up when saw the biscuits and she set up a squawk that made Lex wince until Romy gave her a piece of shortbread to shut her up. This was promptly mangled into a soggy mess, watched in horror by Lex, and Romy rushed into speech in an effort to distract him.

'You never got married.' It was the first thing that came into her head, but as soon as the words came out of her mouth she wished she had stuck with the soggy biscuit.

Lex raised his brows.

'The last time we talked, you said you were going to marry Suzy Stevens,' Romy said with a shade of defiance.

Lex had almost forgotten Suzy. Romy's mother, Molly, had remarried about a year after that week in Paris. As her godson, he had had little choice but to go to the wedding. Romy, of course, had been there too. She had just started her first year at university. After Paris, she had got herself a job in some bar in Avignon. Lex had heard it from his mother, who had heard it from Molly. Romy had had a great time, he had heard.

He had been determined to show Romy that he was over her. Suzy was everything Romy wasn't. She was calm and cool, elegant where Romy was quirky, sophisticated where Romy was passionate. She was suitable in every way.

But she certainly hadn't been stupid. She had seen how Lex looked at Romy, and broken off the relationship when they got back to London that night.

'It didn't work out,' Lex said shortly.

No one had worked out.

'I'm sorry,' said Romy.

'I'm not. It was all for the best.'

Lex's pale grey eyes rested on Freya, still sucking happily on her shortbread. Her fingers were sticky, her face smeared and there were crumbs in her hair and dribbling down her chin.

'I don't want any family responsibilities,' he said. 'I've seen too many people—like Tim today—compromise their careers because of commitments at home. Children are a constant distraction, as far as I can make out. Even a wife expects attention. You can't just stay at work until the job is done. You've got to ring up and explain

and apologise and make up for it by taking yet
more time off… Relationships are too messy and
demanding,' said Lex briskly. 'I long ago came
round to your point of view and decided that
marriage wasn't for me either.'

He looked at Romy. 'It's just as well you
wouldn't marry me. It would have been a disaster
for both of us.'

A disaster. Yes. Romy turned her bangles,
counting them like beads on a rosary. She had
eleven, in a mixture of styles, and she wore them
all together, liking the fact that they were so different and that each came with its own special
memory. Beaten silver. Beaded. Clean and con-
temporary. Ethnic.

One came from the *suq* in Muscat, another from
Mexico. One was a gift from an ex-boyfriend,
another she had bought for herself in Bali.

And *this* one… Romy's fingers lingered on the
silver band. It was inlaid with gold and intricately
carved. An antique.

This one Lex had bought for her at Les Puces,
the famous flea market at the Porte de Clignan-
court. They had spent the morning wandering
around hand in hand, bedazzled by the passion
that had caught them both unawares. Whenever
Romy looked at the bracelet, she remembered
how intensely aware of him she had been, as if

every fibre of her being were attuned to the feel of his fingers around hers, to the hazy excitement of his male, solid body.

A disaster? Maybe. Probably.

She looked up from the bracelet to find Lex watching her, and their eyes met for a brief, jarring moment before she looked quickly away.

'I've never forgotten that week,' she said.

She wondered if Lex was going to tell her that he had, but instead he just said: 'It was a long time ago.'

Well, she couldn't argue with that. She nodded.

'We've both moved on since then,' he said.

Also true. Romy bit her lip. She wasn't quite sure why she was persisting in this, but surely this was a conversation they needed to have?

'I've wanted to talk to you since I've been back, but there never seemed to be an opportunity. I'd thought perhaps at Phin's wedding, but…well, it didn't seem appropriate. And since then, it's been difficult. You're my boss. I didn't think I could just march into your office and demand to speak to you.'

'There's always the phone,' he pointed out unhelpfully. 'Or email.'

'I know. The truth is that I didn't have the nerve,' she said. 'I was really nervous about seeing you today. I know it's stupid, but it seems even more stupid to pretend that there had never been anything between us.'

Romy drew a breath, daunted by Lex's unresponsive expression. 'I just thought that if we could acknowledge it, we would be able to get it out of the way and then stick to business.'

'Fine, let's acknowledge it, then,' said Lex briskly. 'We had a mad week when we were young, but we both know that it would never have lasted longer than that week. Neither of us has any regrets about it. Nobody else knows about it. We've both moved on. What's the problem?'

'No problem, when you put it like that.' But Romy couldn't help feeling a little miffed. Lex was saying everything she had wanted to say, but there was no need for him to sound quite that matter-of-fact about it, was there?

'So now that we've agreed that, we can draw a line underneath the whole episode.'

'Precisely,' she said. 'From now on, our relationship can be purely professional.'

'In that case,' said Lex, opening his computer once more, 'let's go over the main points of the agreement we're offering Willie Grant.'

It was snowing when they landed in Inverness, dry, sleety flakes that spun in the air and did no more than dust the surface of the tarmac. Still, Romy was glad that Summer had arranged for them to hire a solid four wheel drive to take them the rest of the way.

She shivered as she carried Freya down the steps. She'd been living in the tropics for so long that a London winter was shock enough for her system, and she was unprepared for how much colder it would be up here in the north of Scotland. She wished she'd brought a warmer coat.

The vehicle was waiting as arranged just outside the terminal. It was black and substantial and equipped with all the latest technology.

Except a baby seat.

Lex was all ready to get in and drive away until Romy pointed out that Freya would have to travel in the seat, and that it would have to be installed properly.

'It doesn't take long. If you'll just hold her a minute, I'll do it.'

You would think she had asked him to hold a bucket of cold sick.

'I'll install the seat,' he said.

So Romy had to stand there in the cold, while he grew crosser and crosser as he tried to work out how to do it. She tried offering instructions, but Lex ignored her, cursing and muttering under his breath as he searched around for the belt, and then managed to clip it into the wrong buckle, so that he had to start all over again.

He was in a thoroughly bad mood by the time Romy was finally able to buckle Freya in and climb into the passenger seat beside Lex, and matters were not improved when Freya, who had woken as she was laid in the seat, started to grizzle fretfully when they had barely left Inverness.

'What's the matter *now*?' Lex demanded, glowering in the rear view mirror.

Romy looked over her shoulder at her unhappy daughter, then at her watch.

'She's hungry. I am too. Is there any chance we could stop for lunch?'

He sighed impatiently. 'We'll never get there at this rate,' he grumbled, but, according to the sat nav, it would be another two and a half hours before they got to Duncardie, and Lex wasn't sure he could stand the crying another two minutes, let alone two hours.

By the time he saw a hotel up ahead, he was only too happy to pull in. 'But for God's sake, let's be quick about it,' he said as they got out of the car.

To Lex, used to the most exclusive restaurants and the gleaming, high-tech efficiency of Gibson & Grieve's head office, it was something of a surprise to realise that hotels like this still existed. There was a swirly carpet patterned in rich reds and blues, stippled walls painted an unappealing beige and sturdy wooden tables, their legs chipped and worn by generations of feet. Sepia prints were interspersed with the occasional horse brass or jokey tea towel about the joys of golf, and the faint but unmistakable smell of battered fish hung in the air.

On the plus side, it was warm and quiet. Lights flashed on the jukebox in the corner, but it was mercifully silent, and the only other guests were an elderly couple enjoying lunch in the corner. It had a welcoming fire and a friendly landlady who was unfazed by a request for a high chair and was soon deep in discussion with Romy about what Freya would like for her lunch.

Having taken a cursory glance at the menu, Lex ordered a steak and kidney pie and retired to a table by the fire while Romy bore a still-grizzling Freya off to change her nappy. Turning his back on the jolly décor on the wall beside him ("Why is a ship a she?"), Lex rang the office. He got twitchy if he was out of contact and it had been impossible to carry on a conversation on the car phone with Freya bawling in the background.

Not that it was much easier once Romy emerged from the Ladies. Seeing that he was talking to Summer, she carried Freya around the room, jiggling her up and down in her arms and showing her the pictures to distract her from her hunger. The trouble was, she was distracting Lex too. Every time she lifted a hand to point at a picture, her breasts lifted slightly, her back straightened and he seemed ever more unable to block out her shape from the edge of his vision.

It was as if all his senses were on high alert. Romy was wearing loose black trousers and a top in a peacock blue so vibrant that it lit up the entire room, and whenever she turned he was sure he could hear the whisper of the silky material sliding over her skin.

He was sure he could smell her perfume.

Romy was absorbed in her daughter, her face vivid as she chatted away, quite unaware of the fact that whenever she smiled Lex lost track of what Summer was saying.

'Sorry…run that past me again,' he had to ask, not for the first time.

There was a tiny pause. Lex could feel Summer's surprise bouncing up to a satellite and down again. He was famous for the fact that he was always focused and alert. Now Summer would tell Phin that he wasn't concentrating, and Phin would grin and come up with all sorts of ridiculous suggestions as to what might be distracting him.

None of which would be right.

Hunching an irritable shoulder, Lex turned in his chair so that he had his back to Romy.

'I was just wondering how you were getting on with the baby,' Summer said, her voice carefully incurious.

'Fine,' he said shortly. 'Did you warn Grant's people about that?'

'I did. There's absolutely no problem as far as they're concerned.'

'That's something,' he grunted.

The landlady appeared with their lunch at that point, and Romy came back to settle Freya into the high chair, where she started squealing with excitement at the sight of food and banging both her hands on the tray as she bounced up and down. Lex could only imagine how it sounded to Summer in her quiet, calm office as he rang off.

Romy tied a bib on Freya, no easy task when she wouldn't keep still. 'Everything OK at the office?' she asked, mindful of the need to stick to business.

'Yes. Summer has got everything under control.'

'I imagine Summer always does. She's terribly efficient, isn't she?'

'I wouldn't keep her as my PA if she wasn't.'

'Isn't it awkward having your sister-in-law as a PA?' Romy couldn't resist asking as she sat down opposite him and blew on Freya's plate to cool it.

'I'm just glad she wanted to keep on working,' said Lex. 'I don't know how long it'll last. No doubt it'll be a baby next,' he said morosely. 'Then I'll have to train yet another new PA. The wedding was disruptive enough.

'That was my fault for sending her to work for

Phin in the first place,' he remembered, reaching
for the mustard. 'She was supposed to stop him
doing anything stupid, and look what happened!
God knows what she sees in him. They couldn't
be more different.'

Romy had been surprised when she had met
Summer, too. Phin's wife was as crisp as he was
laid-back and charming.

'It must be a case of opposites attract,' she said,
then wished she hadn't. What else had it been
between her and Lex? 'They seem very happy
together, anyway,' she added quickly.

'Yes.'

Why couldn't *he* have fallen in love with
Summer? Lex wondered. She was exactly what he
needed. She was cool and capable, and hated mess
and clutter as much as he did. God only knew
how she coped with Phin's slapdash ways. She
was very pretty, too, although in all honesty Lex
had to admit that he hadn't noticed until Phin
started stirring her up. The transformation had
been quite remarkable.

At last Romy set Freya's plate on the tray of the
high chair and picked up her own knife and fork,
which meant that Lex could start too.

To his relief, Freya stopped squawking instantly and applied herself to her lunch as well.
She was waving a spoon around but her preferred

method of eating seemed to be to squash her fingers into the food and then stick them in her mouth. Lex averted his eyes. He had thought her biscuit eating technique was bad enough. This process was utterly revolting.

Every now and then Romy would load up a second spoon and try to hurry the process along by feeding her, but Freya only pressed her lips together and turned her face stubbornly away.

Romy sighed and laid down the spoon. 'She *will* insist on doing everything herself. I'm afraid it's a slow business. She won't be helped.'

'Like her mother,' said Lex without thinking and then cursed himself as she raised her brows.

'What do you mean?'

'Even as a very small child you refused to hold anyone's hand. You always wanted to do everything by yourself. I remember listening to my mother commiserating with yours about how independent you were.'

'I'd forgotten that.' Romy pushed the spoon hopefully in Freya's direction once more. 'I've always assumed I only realised how important it was to be independent after my father left, but maybe I was born that way.'

'Stubborn,' Lex agreed.

'You know, you're not exactly Mr Malleable,' she pointed out.

'I always did what my parents expected me to,' he said with a trace of bitterness. 'I had to be the sensible, responsible one, unlike you and Phin, who gaily went your own way. I used to envy how adventurous you both were,' he confessed, even as he marvelled at how easily he had strayed away from business. 'Neither of you ever seemed to be afraid of anything.'

'Dogs,' Romy reminded him. She had been badly bitten by a collie when she was five and had been very nervous of dogs ever since.

'All right, anything except dogs,' Lex conceded. 'And commitment, of course,' he added smoothly. 'Neither of you ever liked to be tied down to a plan either.'

'And yet there's Phin married,' said Romy, 'and here's me with a baby. It's funny the way life works out, isn't it?'

'Yes,' said Lex, thinking about the twists and turns that had brought them both to this shabby pub. 'Very funny.'

The elderly couple in the corner had finished their lunch, and stopped at the table on their way past.

'What a lovely baby!' The woman beamed and chucked Freya's cheek. 'Aren't you the bonny one?'

Intent on her lunch, Freya paid little attention, but Lex felt his jaw sag.

Lovely? In disbelief, he looked at the baby in

question, who was happily rubbing mashed potato into her hair. One ear appeared to be encrusted with carrot and he didn't even want to think about what might be dribbling from her nose.

Romy avoided his eyes. 'Thank you,' she said with a smile.

'I'll bet she can twist you round her little finger, eh?' The man actually *nudged* Lex. 'Wait till she's older. She won't give you a moment's peace!'

'Make the most of it while she's small.' His wife nodded at Lex, who was too dumbfounded to do more than stare back at her. 'You've got a lovely wee family,' she told him. 'You're a lucky man!'

'Enjoy your lunch.' Her husband nodded farewell as he took her arm.

A gust of cold air swirled into the room as they opened the door, but the next moment it had swung to, and Lex and Romy were left alone in the dining room.

There was a moment of utter silence, and then Romy dissolved into helpless laughter. Diverted from her lunch, Freya stared at her mother, and started to chuckle as well, clearly puzzled by all the merriment, but perfectly happy to join in.

'What's so funny?' demanded Lex, looking from one to the other.

'Your expression,' Romy managed at last, wiping her eyes and drawing a shuddery breath.

'I wish you could have seen yourself! I've never seen anyone look so appalled at the thought of being associated with a *lovely wee family*!'

Her whole face was alight with humour. The dark eyes were sparkling with laughter, and her expression was so vivid that Lex's heart tripped, and all at once he was back in that restaurant in Paris, drinking in the sight of her, dazzled by her warmth and her beauty.

He made himself look away. 'I've never been taken for a father before,' he said, his voice desert dry. 'I've always assumed it would be obvious that I wasn't.'

'It's an easy enough mistake to make,' said Romy. 'We must look like an ordinary family.'

CHAPTER THREE

'I SUPPOSE SO.' For some reason, the thought made Lex uneasy. He felt ridiculously thrown. He wanted to rush after the couple and ask them how they could possibly have thought that he was Freya's father. What did he need to do? Have *never in a million years* tattooed across his forehead?

Romy's smile still curved her mouth as she picked up her knife and fork once more. 'I don't think they were very impressed by your hands-off approach, though. I could see them watching you while I was trying to entertain Freya. They obviously thought you should have been helping me instead of making phone calls. I suspect that was why she thought she should remind you how lucky you are to have us.'

'Dear God.' Lex glanced at Freya, who had gone back to smearing lunch over her face, and shuddered. 'I'm glad to have amused you,' he added austerely when Romy started to giggle again.

'Oh, you have. It was worth the rush this morning just to see you!'

Freya was clearly a baby who enjoyed her food. There was a lot of gurgling and squealing and squeaking, with much smacking of lips together and banging of spoons. And the mess…indescribable! Lex decided, eyeing Freya askance as he put his knife and fork together.

'I just hope she's not going to be eating in front of Willie Grant!'

'Don't worry,' Romy soothed. 'I'll make sure he knows you're not responsible for her in any way.'

Lex pushed his plate aside. 'Who *is* responsible for her, Romy?'

'I am,' she said instantly.

It was none of his business, Lex knew, but he couldn't help asking. 'What about her father?'

The last amusement faded from Romy's face. 'I thought we were sticking to business?' she said, disliking the defensive note in her voice. She busied herself filling the spoon and offering it, without much hope, to Freya, who took it and wiped it on her nose.

He shrugged. 'I'm just interested in why you're having to do everything yourself.'

'Because I want to.'

Edgy now, Romy picked up her mat. It showed an unlikely hunting scene, with red-coated riders hallooing and urging their horses over a hedge, while the hounds bounded alongside. In spite of herself, Romy shrank a little at the sight of their lolling tongues and great paws. No one would think of putting spiders or snakes on a mat, would they? So why were dogs different? If she had noticed the dogs before, she wouldn't have enjoyed her pie nearly so much.

She twisted the mat around so that they faced Lex instead.

'Doesn't he get a say?'

'He doesn't know.' Romy balanced the mat between her hands, turned it so that it sat on the shorter edge. 'I haven't told him yet.'

'He doesn't *know*?' said Lex, incredulous.

'Look, it was just a fling,' she said, not looking at him. 'A holiday romance. I was running a dive centre in Sulawesi, Michael was travelling… He's an artist, very laid-back, very charming.'

Very everything Lex wasn't.

Round went the mat. 'We had a good time. Neither of us wanted any more than that. Michael was on the rebound. He'd been dumped by his girlfriend a couple of months earlier, and I…well, you know how I feel about commitment.'

Romy looked up then, and looked straight at Lex. The pale eyes were shuttered, his expression indecipherable.

'It wasn't just you, Lex,' she said, since they seemed to have abandoned the pretence of sticking to business. 'I don't want to marry anyone. I certainly didn't want to marry Michael. It was never a big deal for either of us. I liked him—he was great—but there was never any question of anything more than that.'

'So how did Freya happen?' asked Lex.

'The usual way,' said Romy with a touch of her old tartness. Then, when he just met her gaze, she bit her lip and went on. 'We took precautions of course, but…well, sometimes it happens. By the time I realised that I was pregnant, Michael had already left.

'He sent an email when he got home, just to say hello, but I knew that he wasn't interested in me beyond a fling. I had another message a couple of months later, telling me that he was back with his girlfriend, so an email from me saying that he was going to be a father would have been the last thing he wanted.'

Lex frowned. 'Wouldn't he want to know anyway?'

'I don't know…' Romy sighed. 'Sometimes I thought he would, and that it was wrong not to tell him, but then I thought of him being with his girlfriend, and I didn't want to spoil that for him. It's not as if he made any promises. Michael talked about Kate a lot when we were together, so I know how much he wanted to be with her. When he emailed, he sounded so happy—'

She broke off, flashing Lex a look. 'Would *you* have wanted to know?' she asked abruptly.

'Yes.'

'Just like that? No thought about how having a child would turn your life upside down?'

'I'd still want to know,' said Lex. 'If, after Paris…' He didn't finish the sentence, but she knew what he was thinking. 'I'd have wanted to know,' he said. 'I'd have thought I had the right to know.'

Romy eyed him in dismay. Of all the people she would have expected to understand, she had thought it would be Lex! Lex, who hated chaos and was clearly appalled by Freya.

'Maybe I was wrong,' she said, chewing her lip. 'It just seemed to me that learning that you're a father is such a big thing. Having a child…it changes everything. *Everything.* I imagined how I would feel if I was Kate, finding out that it wasn't just Michael any more, but Michael and a baby. It would have changed things for her too… Oh, I've been round and round about this so many times since I found out I was pregnant!'

Tiring of the mat, Romy let it drop to the table and started fiddling with a spoon instead, spinning it slowly between her finger and thumb. 'Should

I tell Michael? Should I not? What if he didn't want anything to do with Freya? What would that do to her, to know that her father never wanted her? Would that be better or worse than not having a father at all?'

'That's not really the point,' said Lex severely. 'The point is that this Michael is partly responsible for her, and that means he should help support her.'

'I don't want help,' said Romy stubbornly. 'I don't need it.'

She caught the echo of her own words about Freya, and grimaced a little. 'I don't want to rely on anyone,' she tried to explain. 'It was my choice to have a child, my choice to bring her up on my own. Telling Michael wouldn't be about the money.'

She had begun to irritate herself with her fiddling and she made herself stop and put her hands in her lap. 'I expect he would want to support Freya if he knew,' she said. 'Michael's a decent man. He wouldn't run away from the responsibility.

'I'm the one that has done the running away,' she admitted. 'I didn't want to upset things between him and Kate, but the truth is that I used that as an excuse. I was afraid that if I told Michael he might want to be involved in Freya's life. He might want to see her, and she…she might love him.'

Romy's eyes rested on Freya, who was absently

wiping a spoon in her hair and wearing a pensive expression. 'Children do love their fathers.'

Her voice was very sad, and Lex's expression changed. 'There's no reason to think that he would be like your father, Romy.'

'No, but what if he was? What if he disappointed her? What if he didn't love her the way she deserves to be loved?'

She had been such a daddy's girl. Her whole world had revolved around her father. She couldn't wait for him to come home at night and drove her mother mad, jiggling up and down with excitement. There was no joy to compare with that of seeing him appear, of running into his arms, of being swept up into a hug and swung round and round until she was giddy and giggling.

'Who's my best girl?' he would ask.

Romy would shriek, 'Me! Me!'

'And who do I love best in the world?'

'Me!'

Romy could still remember it, the blinding happiness, the utter, utter security of wrapping her skinny arms around his neck and knowing that her father was home and that nothing could go wrong when he was there.

And then one day he sat her down and told her that he would never be coming home again. That he was going to live with someone who was not her mother and have a new family. She was going to have a new brother or sister, he told her.

'But I still love you,' he said.

Romy didn't believe him. If he loved her, he wouldn't leave her. She was six, and she never felt quite safe again. Even now, the memory of that morning had the power to rip at her heart and bring back the black slap of disbelief. How could he have done that to her? How could he have left his best girl?

Twenty-four years ago, and it still made her feel sick with misery and incomprehension.

The thought that Freya might be hurt in the same way was unbearable. However hard it might be to struggle on her own, Romy knew it was better than letting herself rely on someone who might leave them both.

'It wasn't an easy decision, Lex,' she said slowly. 'I thought about it every day. I still think about it. I don't know if I did the right thing not telling Michael when I was first pregnant. It *felt* right, that's all I can say. It felt as if it would be better for Freya if it was just two of us.

'Recently though…I suppose it's partly seeing Tim and realising that there are great fathers out there, but I've been thinking that I should tell Michael about Freya after all. Not for the money, but because Freya needs a father as well as me.

And because Michael deserves to know that he has a daughter.

'But first I want to be sure I'm truly independent. This deal with Grant's Supersavers is important to you, I know,' she told Lex, 'but it's just as important to me. It's my chance to really make my mark, something really impressive to put on my CV for when I have to look for my next job. In the past, I've just drifted from country to country and picked up work when I needed it, but it's different now. I need a proper job, and I can't rely on anyone but myself for that.'

'You're not exactly alone in the world,' Lex pointed out.

'No,' she acknowledged. 'Mum and Keith were great when I came home to have Freya, but they've done enough. They're too old to live with a baby. I moved out as soon as I could, but I was getting desperate about finding anything when Phin offered me this job at Gibson & Grieve.'

Romy looked across the table at Lex. 'I never thanked you for that.'

'Thank Phin,' he said with a dismissive gesture. 'He fixed it all.'

'You're Chief Executive. You could have said no.'

'I wouldn't have done that,' said Lex, but he avoided her eyes, remembering how dismayed he had been when Phin had told him what he had done. If he thought he could have persuaded his brother to change his mind, he would have done.

'Well, thank you anyway.'

'You can thank me by making sure this deal goes through,' said Lex roughly, and Romy nodded.

'I'll do whatever I can to make it happen,' she said. 'For both of us. And when it's done, and I've got the experience I need to get a permanent job, then I'll tell Michael that he has a daughter.'

The snow was little more than a light powder when they left the pub, but the further they drove, the heavier it got, until great, fat flakes were swirling around the car and splattering onto the windscreen.

The short winter afternoon was drawing in, too, and Romy began to feel as if they were trapped in one of the snow scenes she had loved to shake as a child, except in this one the snow didn't settle after a minute or two. It just kept on coming. Soon, Romy couldn't see the country they were driving through, but it felt dark and empty and wild, and it was miles since they had passed a vehicle going the other way.

'Do you think we should turn back?' she ventured at last.

'Turn back? What for?'

'The snow's very heavy. What if we get stuck?'

'We're not going to get stuck,' said Lex. 'We're certainly not turning round and going back on the off chance that we do. We're almost there. This meeting is too important to miss because of "what if".'

'We might break down,' said Romy, who had been checking her mobile. 'And I'm not getting a signal on my phone. How would we get help?'

Lex sucked in a breath. 'Romy, there is nothing wrong with the car,' he said, keeping his voice even with an effort. 'Anyway, I thought you were the one who wanted adventure? When did you turn into a worrier?'

'When I became a mother,' said Romy, glancing over her shoulder to where Freya was, thankfully, sound asleep. 'I used to pack up and go without a thought. It never occurred to me that anything could go wrong, but now…'

She sat back in the seat, turning the useless phone between her hands, her eyes fixed on the swirling snow but her mind on the day her life had changed for ever.

'I didn't know what terror was until Freya was born,' she said slowly after a moment. 'Until I held her in my arms and looked into her face, and realised that it was up to me to keep her safe and well and happy. What if I can't do it? What if I get it all wrong? I'm terrified that I'll be a bad mother.'

Where had *that* come from? Romy wondered, startled. She spent a lot of time assuring her mother and her friends that she was fine on her own, that she was managing perfectly well. She spent a lot of time telling herself that too.

And she *was* fine. She *was* managing. She just didn't tell anyone how hard it was. How scared she was.

Now, unaccountably, she had told Lex, of all people. The one person who would least understand.

'I worry about everything now,' she confessed. 'I worry about what will happen if Freya is sick or if she struggles at school. How will I pay for her university fees? What if she has a boyfriend who hurts her?'

Lex shot her a disbelieving look. 'It's a bit early to worry about that, isn't it?' he said. 'She's only a baby.'

'Thirteen months,' Romy told him, 'and growing every day. I know it's stupid, but I can't help myself. I'm afraid I won't be a good enough mother, that I won't be able to give her what she needs. I'm afraid I won't be able to support her by myself, and that I'll have to rely on other people, that her happiness will be in someone else's hands. I'm afraid her father will want to be part of her life and afraid that he won't. Oh, yes,' she said with a lopsided smile, 'I'm a real scaredy cat now!'

'Then you've changed more than I thought you had.'

'You should be glad. An irresponsible eighteen-year-old with itchy feet isn't much good to you.' Romy paused. 'She never was.'

'No,' Lex agreed, and his voice was tinder dry.

Romy blew out a long breath. 'I miss being that girl sometimes,' she said. 'I miss how fearless I was. I had such a good time. I can't believe I did all those things now, now that I'm scared and sensible and the kind of person who puts on a suit to go into work every day. It feels like remembering a different person altogether.'

'So if you hadn't got pregnant, would you still be drifting?'

'Probably. I'd been in Indonesia a couple of years. I was thinking of moving on. Thailand, maybe. Or Vietnam. Instead I'm a single mother living in the suburbs and struggling into work on the tube every day.'

Lex glanced at her, and then away. 'No regrets?'

Romy looked over her shoulder again. Freya's head was lolling to one side. Ridiculously long lashes fanned her cheeks and her lips were parted over a bubble of dribble. Her baby. Her daughter. Her best girl.

'No,' she said. 'No regrets.'

They drove on through the dark in silence. In spite of her earlier anxiety about the snow, deep down

Romy wasn't really worried. There was something infinitely reassuring about Lex's coolly
competent presence. He drove the way he did everything else, like a man utterly sure of himself.
The only time he lost that sense of assurance was
in the air, but now he was on the ground and firmly
back in control.

Romy eyed him under her lashes. His hands
were big and capable on the steering wheel, and
the muted light from the dashboard threw the cool
planes and austere angles of his face into relief.

That was the point she should have looked
away, but her gaze came to rest on his mouth
instead, and without warning the memory of how
it felt against hers set something dangerous strumming deep inside her.

Alarmed, she forced her eyes away, but instead
of doing something sensible like fixing on the
satellite navigation screen, they skittered back to
his hands, which only made the strumming worse
as the memories she had kept repressed for so
long clamoured for release.

Lex's hands. The feel of them was imprinted on
her skin. He had long dextrous fingers that had
sent heat flooding through her. They had been
warm skimming over the curve of her hip, sliding
over her thigh, gentle up her spine, hungry at her
breast… He had played her body like an instru-

ment, coaxing the wild, wondrous excitement with those possessive hands, that mouth, exploring her, loving her, unwrapping her, unlocking her as if she were some magical gift.

Desperately, Romy made herself stare out at the snow until the swirling flakes made her giddy. Or perhaps it was the memories doing that. Why had she let herself remember? She should have kept them firmly locked away, the way Lex had clearly done.

Now she was hot and prickly all over, and even the backs of her knees were tingling as if he had just kissed her there again.

He had been such an unexpected lover, so cool on the surface, so passionate below. Afterwards, Romy had realised that it shouldn't have been such a surprise. As a child, she had once seen Lex play the piano, had watched astounded as he drew the most incredible music from the keys.

Her mother had claimed that he was good enough to play professionally. There had been a flaming row with his father when Gerald Gibson had dismissed Lex's talent.

'He can play the piano if he wants, but what's the point of him studying music?' he demanded. 'Lex will be joining Gibson & Grieve. Economics makes much more sense.'

What Lex thought about the piano, Romy had

never known. Only once more had she ever heard him play, in a dimly lit café in some Paris back street, which they had found quite by accident. They had sat late into the night, listening to the band.

Occasionally one of the musicians had drifted off for a drink, and someone from the audience would get up and play in their place. Lex had taken a turn at the piano at last, improvising with a guy on the saxophone, his body moving in time to the music, utterly absorbed, and Romy had listened, her throat aching with inexplicable tears. This was not the dutiful son, the boy who had joined the family firm and set out to please his father. This was her lover and a man she suspected Gerald Gibson didn't even know existed.

'Romy?'

Lex's voice startled Romy out of her thoughts and she jerked upright. 'What?'

'I wondered if you'd fallen asleep.'

'No. I was…thinking.'

'What about?'

For a moment, a very brief moment, Romy considered telling him the truth. She could turn to him in the darkness and confess that she had been thinking about him, about how he made music and how he made love and how he had made her feel.

But the thought had barely crossed her mind before she remembered how his face had closed on the plane. 'It was a long time ago,' he had said. 'We've both moved on.'

As they had. Lex was right. It was pointless to bring it all up again.

He wanted to draw a line under the whole episode and stick to business. And let's remember, Romy, she reminded herself, this is your boss, and you need this job. If he wants to stick to business, business it is.

'Nothing,' she said.

'Well, start thinking about how you're going to explain Freya's presence to Grant.' Lex tapped the sat nav. 'According to this, we're nearly there.'

Sure enough, a few minutes later they were bumping along a track and over a bridge, and then quite suddenly there were lights glimmering through the snow and the dark bulk of Duncardie was looming above them.

Concealing his relief at having arrived at last, Lex drove into a courtyard, and parked as close as he could to the massive front door.

'Only three and a half hours late,' he said grimly.

He switched off the engine, and there was a sudden, crushing silence, broken only by the sound of Freya burbling to herself in the back seat. She had woken half an hour before, and Romy had been on tenterhooks in case she started to cry again, but her daughter seemed perfectly content to play with her toes and chat away in her own incomprehensible language.

'OK,' said Lex. 'Now remember, the whole deal is riding on this meeting, so we've got to get it right.'

'Right,' said Romy.

'If we want Grant to take us seriously, we'll have to be professional, and that means making a good impression right from the start. We're going to have to work hard to make up for turning up late with the entire contents of a Mothercare catalogue.'

'Professional,' Romy agreed. 'Absolutely.'

The moment the wipers had stilled, the snow had started to build up on the windscreen, and already they could barely see through it.

Lex was calculating how quickly he could unload the car. 'You take Freya,' he told Romy. 'I'll bring the stuff.'

Romy thought doubtfully of everything she had brought with her. 'It'll take ages if you do it on your own. Why don't we do it together?'

'There's no point in two of us blundering around in the snow,' he said gruffly. 'Take Freya into the warm. Hopefully we'll have a chance to change and get rid of all this clobber before we meet Grant himself.'

'All right.' Romy drew a breath and looked at Lex. 'I'm ready.'

He nodded and reached for the door handle.
'Then let's go and get this deal.'

It wasn't far to the door, but it was bitterly cold
and to Lex, labouring backwards and forwards in
the dark through the snow, it felt as if he were
trapped in an endless blizzard. Head down, he
dumped stuff in the stone porch as quickly as he
could before running back for the next load. At
least someone was transferring it all inside, he
saw, but he was very glad indeed to make the last
trip, skidding and sliding over the snow.

Brushing the worst of the snow off himself in
the porch, Lex shook out his sodden trousers with
an irritable grimace. His feet were frozen, his
hands numb, and melting snow was trickling
down his neck, and he was cursing Willie Grant's
refusal to go to London and meet in a warm, dry
office, where all sensible deals were made.

But this was the deal he wanted, Lex reminded
himself. He bent to retrieve the last of Freya's
luggage and stepped through the door.

He found himself in a vast, baronial hall,
complete with antlers on the wall, some sad,
glassy-eyed creatures stuffed and mounted long
ago, and even the requisite suit of armour standing
to attention at the foot of a magnificent staircase.

Lex didn't see any of them. He registered
three things simultaneously. One, a small, portly

man with a halo of white hair, holding Freya. Willie Grant himself, in fact, who turned to watch Lex's approach.

Two, the fact that he, Lex, far from presenting a crisply professional appearance, was dripping snow everywhere and had a bright yellow bag decorated with teddy bears wearing bow ties in one hand and a huge pack of nappies and a push-chair in the other.

And three, Romy, terrified and trying not to show it, standing rigidly beside Willie Grant while an Irish Wolfhound, easily the biggest dog Lex had ever seen, sniffed interestedly at Freya's feet.

Forgetting his humiliating appearance, Lex dropped the teddy bear bag and snapped his fingers. 'Come,' he said to the dog, who trotted obediently over to greet him.

'Sit.'

The great rump sank to the floor.

'Good dog,' said Lex, and rubbed the huge head that came up to his chest, while Romy sent him a speaking look of gratitude.

Willie Grant's expression was harder to decipher.

'That's Magnus,' he said. 'He doesn't usually go to strangers.'

'I like dogs,' said Lex, giving Magnus a final pat.

It was too late to hide the pushchair and nappies. He set them down, tried to pretend that he wasn't dripping everywhere, and stepped forward to offer his hand.

'Lex Gibson,' he introduced himself.

'Willie Grant.' Willie's grip was firm and he studied Lex with interest, not unmixed with surprise.

'I'm very sorry we're so late.'

'Oh, not to worry about that,' said Willie. 'Your secretary rang, so we got the message that you would be delayed and that you were bringing the wee lassie with you.' He beamed at Freya and tweaked her nose. 'She's a bonny one, isn't she?'

'Yes, I'm sorry about that—' Lex began, and then stopped short as Freya, clearly recognising him, broke into a gummy smile and reached out her arms towards him.

Instinctively, Lex took a step back, but Willie was watching Freya and didn't notice. 'Ah, I see who *you* want!' he chuckled. 'Old Willie's not good enough for you, is he?'

And before Lex could react, he had handed Freya over and turned to take Romy by the arm.

'Now come away in and have some tea in the library,' he said and bore her off up the magnificent stone staircase, leaving Lex, aghast, holding Freya at rigid arm's length.

It wasn't often that Lex was at a loss for words.

'Er…' was the best he could manage.

'Perhaps I should take Freya,' Romy said quickly, trying to hang back. 'Lex is rather wet.'

But Willie wasn't to be deflected. 'Oh, bring the wee one too, of course,' he tossed over his shoulder at Lex. 'You'll soon dry off by a good fire. Ewan's around here somewhere. He'll take your stuff to your room while Elspeth's bringing us some tea.'

That left Lex with little choice but to carry Freya gingerly after them, dangling between his hands. He was terrified that she was going to cry, but she just stared at him with those disconcertingly direct dark eyes.

The library was warm and cluttered, with heavy red velvet curtains closed against the night and a fire crackling behind a guard.

'We put that up as soon as we heard you were bringing the baby,' said Willie.

'I was afraid she'd be a nuisance,' Romy said, settling herself on the red leather sofa, and looking anxiously over her shoulder to see where Lex and Freya were.

To her dismay, the huge dog had followed them up the stairs and threw itself down on the rug in front of the fire with a great thud. Romy was convinced she could feel a tremor in the floor and wouldn't have been in the least surprised if the ornaments had come crashing off the mantelpiece at the impact.

She had been terrified in the hall when Magnus appeared. On one level, Romy knew it was stupid. Just because one dog had bitten her when she was a child didn't mean that every dog would bite. Perhaps it was knowing that they *could* that made her so nervous.

And this dog was a monster, the size of a small pony at least. When it had stuck its great muzzle towards her, she had frozen with terror. Unable to move, the breath clicking frantically in her throat, she had only been able to watch as it swung its head round to investigate Freya in Willie's arms. Her daughter's feet had been mere inches away from those huge teeth.

Willie didn't seem to have noticed anything amiss. He'd been laughing with Freya, as if unaware that a mere nudge from the beast beside him could send them both crashing to the ground where it could savage them.

She should snatch Freya back, Romy had thought frantically, but that would mean pushing past the dog and panic had clogged her throat at the idea of touching it. What if it turned on her? What if its eyes went red and it went for her? What if—?

And then Lex had stepped into the hall, and the world had miraculously righted. He had taken in the situation at a glance. Romy had sagged with relief as he'd called the dog away. His effortless control of the animal had given her a queer thrill, she had to admit, even as she despised herself for feeling so safe with him. That smacked too much of neediness for one of Romy's independent turn of mind.

Still, there was no denying that Lex was a formidable figure, even dripping snow and burdened with ridiculous bags. He must have hated meeting Willie like that, Romy thought, remembering how much he had wanted to present a professional image.

It was all her fault for bringing so much stuff with her. Well, she would make it up to him, Romy vowed. She would do everything she could to make sure Willie agreed to sell to Lex.

Wondering where Lex and Freya had got to, Romy made herself focus on Willie, who was assuring her that Freya would be no trouble. 'I like to see the wee ones,' he told her. 'Moira and I dreamed of Duncardie full of children, but sadly it wasn't to be.'

'I'm sorry,' said Romy gently.

Willie looked sad, but squared his shoulders. 'At least we had each other,' he remembered. 'I never looked at another woman after I met Moira.'

'You must miss her very much.'

'I do. It's been five years now, and I still miss her every day. And every day I remember how lucky I was to have found her. It's a great thing to find a love like that,' he told Romy.

'It must be.'

Fleetingly, Romy found herself thinking about Lex, which was ridiculous, really, because although that week in Paris had been wonderful and intense, it hadn't been about love, not the way Willie meant. It had been passion, it had been desire, it had been sheer, unadulterated lust, but it couldn't have been *love*.

She hadn't wanted it to be love. Even at eighteen, she had known that love meant making compromises. It meant putting your heart and your happiness into someone else's hands, and Romy had done that once. She had loved her father absolutely, and she wasn't prepared to risk her heart again.

Never again.

CHAPTER FOUR

WILLIE was bustling around the tea tray when Lex appeared at last. He was walking very gingerly and holding Freya as if she were a grenade with a very wobbly pin. He must have come up those stairs very, very slowly.

Evidently forgetting his new family-friendly image, Lex handed Freya over with such an anguished grimace that Romy had to tuck in the corners of her mouth quite firmly to stop herself laughing. Fortunately, Willie was busy with the teapot and didn't notice.

'You must be frozen,' she said tactfully instead.

'Yes, indeed.' Willie looked up. 'Come and dry yourself by the fire, Lex. Just push Magnus out of the way.'

Romy thought it would take a bulldozer to move a dog that size, but Lex just clicked his tongue and pointed and Magnus heaved himself to one side with a sigh.

'I didn't have you down as a dog man,' said Willie, handing him a cup of tea.

Lex nodded his thanks. 'It's not the sort of thing that normally comes up in the business world.'

'I think it should. It helps to know who you're dealing with and so far, you've been something of an unknown entity. Oh, I know you're a canny enough businessman,' Willie went on as Lex opened his mouth to speak, 'but beyond that, there's not much information out there about what you're like as a person.'

'I don't like to mix my personal life with business,' said Lex stiffly.

'Fair enough,' Willie allowed, 'but I like to get to know a man before I decide whether we can do business or not.'

'I understand that.' There was a suspicion of clenched teeth in Lex's voice, and Romy could see a muscle jumping in his cheek.

She held her breath. Lex's temper, never the longest, would be on a very short fuse after the day he had had. He hated being out of control, and things had gone from bad to worse, with Tim unable to make it, a long delay until she turned up, and Romy didn't suppose he had been pleased to discover that he would be spending the following forty-eight hours with someone he had been comprehensively ignoring ever since she had started work. On top of all that, he'd been landed with a baby, forced to confront his fear of flying and had to drive through a blizzard. Small wonder if he was irritable now.

But in the end all he said was, 'That's why we're here.'

'Quite,' said Willie comfortably as he took a seat in a wing chair. His eyes, bright blue, rested speculatively on Lex's rigid face. 'I suggest we talk about the deal over dinner tonight. Enjoy your tea for now.'

Romy suspected the chance of Lex enjoying his tea was slight. Willie's personal approach to negotiations was not at all Lex's style. He was much happier in the boardroom, talking figures with hard-headed men in suits. Gibson & Grieve's Chief Executive had many strengths, but chatting sociably by a fire wasn't one of them.

At least here she could help. Romy might not be sufficiently ruthless when it came to negotiating, but she had advanced social skills.

'How old is the castle?' she asked, drawing Willie's attention away from Lex and setting out to charm him.

It wasn't difficult. Willie had been closely involved in setting up the negotiations. Unlike Lex, he liked to deal with the details himself and had been perfectly happy to talk to Romy, who was far from being the most senior member of the acquisitions team. They had already established a rapport on the phone and by email, and she had been touched by the warmth of his welcome. He had seemed genuinely delighted to meet Freya, too.

How Willie felt about Lex was less clear. Chatting away to Romy, he was studying him without appearing to do so, the shrewd blue eyes faintly puzzled.

Lex himself was starting to steam by the fire, and he stepped away, conceding the prime space on the rug to Magnus, who immediately reclaimed it.

Before he could choose a seat, Willie, in mid history, waved him to the sofa next to Romy. It would have been churlish to have opted for the other chair, so Lex had little choice but to sit down next to her, Freya wriggling between them.

Over the baby's head, his eyes met Romy's briefly. Hers were gleaming with laughter at his reluctance, or perhaps at the absurdity of the whole situation, and in spite of himself Lex, who had been feeling distinctly irritable, felt an answering smile tug at his mouth.

Though, God knew, there was little enough to smile about. His feet were so cold, he had lost all feeling in his toes, and his trousers were still clammy and uncomfortable. He had sensed

Willie's reservation about him, too, and it didn't bode well for the negotiations.

Romy, though, was doing a fantastic job of charming the old devil. Lex contributed little to the conversation. He couldn't do small talk and, besides, how could he be expected to concentrate on lairds and battles and licences to crenellate when Freya was rolling around on the shiny leather, and beyond her Romy was leaning forward, listening to Willie. When her face was animated, when the firelight burnished the dark, silky hair and warmed the lovely curve of her mouth, of her throat.

Lex was still grappling with the fact that after twelve years of trying to forget her, she was actually there, warm and bright and as beautiful as ever, her vivid presence still with the power to send his senses tumbling around as if they were trapped in some invisible washing machine. The moment he managed to steady them by grasping onto a sensible fact, or remembering the deal and everything that rested upon it, Romy would smile or turn her head and off they would go again, looping and swirling until it was all he could do to string two words together.

It was most disconcerting, and the last thing Lex needed right then. He gripped his cup and saucer, holding them well out of Freya's reach, and wished, not for the first time, that Tim's son had chosen any day other than this to have his crisis.

Freya struggled towards him once more, preparing to clamber over him, and protested loudly when Romy scooped her away.

'Why don't you put her on the floor?' Willie asked.

'What about the dog?'

'Oh, Magnus won't mind.'

Lex could see that whether the dog minded or not was the least of Romy's concerns. 'I'll keep an eye on her,' he said gruffly.

Of course, the moment she was allowed down, Freya made a beeline for the dog, but Lex was there before her, catching her in one arm and making careful introductions between dog and baby. Freya squealed with excitement when Magnus sniffed her cautiously, and Lex showed her how to stroke the wiry head, but she soon lost interest and set off to explore the rest of the room while he sat in an armchair, relieved to have distanced himself from the heady sense of Romy's nearness, but nervous about the baby. Willie and Romy were so deep in conversation that it was obviously up to him to keep an eye on her, and it was a nerve-racking business.

For a start, Freya could crawl with alarming speed, and she was never still. One minute she was all over the dog, the next patting Willie's slippers.

She tried to haul herself upright on an armchair, only to lose her balance and plump back down on her bottom. Undaunted, she tried again, and this time stayed upright long enough to take one or two wobbly steps while holding onto the cushion.

She would be walking soon, Lex guessed, and he was glad to think he wouldn't be responsible for her then. You wouldn't have a moment's peace. Look how quick she was on all fours. Now she was crawling back to the chair where Lex sat and tugging at his damp trousers to pull herself up against his knees. The creases in them would never be the same again. Lex tried to edge his legs out of her reach, but Freya's little fingers held tight, and, short of kicking her away from him, he was stuck and had to sit there while she treated him as another piece of furniture and manoeuvred unsteadily around him.

Meanwhile, Romy and Willie were getting on like fire in a match factory. Perhaps this visit wasn't going to be such a disaster after all. Watching Willie Grant laughing with Romy, Lex found it hard to believe he was going to turn round and refuse the deal. One wary eye on Freya, Lex let himself relax slightly and imagine the moment when he could announce to his father that the deal was secured, and that Gibson & Grieve had a foothold in Scotland at last.

And then?

Uneasily, Lex pushed the question aside. He had been planning this deal for a year now. Once this deal was done, there would be others, hopefully not involving a baby. Romy would find a new job. Life would go back to normal.

It would be fine.

Lex had lost track of the conversation between Willie and Romy entirely when Willie hoisted himself to his feet.

'You don't mind if we abandon you for a few minutes, do you, Lex? We won't be long.'

'Of course not.' Courteously Lex got to his feet, hoping he hadn't missed out on some vital conversation. Willie clearly wasn't expecting him to go with them, though, and Lex was delighted at the thought of a few minutes on his own. 'I'll be very happy to stay here and keep an eye on the fire.'

'Excellent.' Willie moved to the door. 'Magnus will keep you company. He doesn't like the stairs. Shall we go then, Romy? Oh, I don't think you'll want to take Freya, will you?' he added as Romy bent to pick up her daughter. 'It's chilly up there, and you might find the spiral stairs a bit tricky with her.'

'Oh.' Already by the door with Freya in her arms, Romy hesitated.

Willie flicked Freya's nose. 'You'd rather stay with your daddy, wouldn't you, precious?'

Daddy?

Lex opened his mouth, but Romy got in first. 'Er, Lex isn't actually Freya's father,' she said.

'Isn't he now?' Willie's brows shot up. He eyed Lex narrowly, and then gave a small approving nod, 'Well, that makes me think the better of you.'

Mystified, Lex looked at Romy, who could only lift her brows with a tiny shrug to show that she was as puzzled as he was.

'We won't be long, Lex.' Willie held the door open for Romy, who threw Lex an agonised glance. She could hardly insist on taking Freya with her against Willie's advice, he realised.

Heart sinking, Lex went over and she handed the baby over with a speaking glance. 'I won't be long,' she promised.

Freya watched the door close behind her mother and belatedly realised that she had been abandoned. Her eyes narrowed in outrage and she let out a bellow of outrage that startled Lex so much that he nearly dropped her.

'She'll be back as soon as she can,' he said with desperation, but Freya only opened her mouth to wail in earnest.

'Oh, God…oh, God…' Frantically, he jiggled her up and down, and for a moment he thought it would work. Freya definitely paused in mid-wail, and Lex could practically see her considering whether she was distracted enough to stop crying altogether, but she evidently decided that she wasn't ready to be consoled just yet because off she went again, at ear-splitting volume.

'Shh…. Shh…' Lex had a sudden vision of Romy walking Freya around the pub at lunchtime, so he set off around the room, jiggling the baby awkwardly as he went.

To his astonishment, this seemed to do the trick. Freya's screams subsided to snuffly sobs, and then stopped altogether.

Perhaps there wasn't so much to this baby business, after all? Obviously, the child just needed a firm hand.

Bored of circling the library, Lex stopped and put Freya on the carpet. She promptly started yelling again until he picked her up again, at which point the noise miraculously stopped.

A firm hand. Right.

Lex set off on another circuit of the library.

He was on his fifth when the door opened. He looked round, hoping it would be Romy, but instead it was Elspeth, the housekeeper, who had come to clear the tea tray.

'The wee one must be tired,' she said, noting the long lashes spiky with tears and the hectic flush in the baby's cheeks. And Lex's harassed expression. 'Would you like me to show you to your room?'

At least it would make a change from the

library, thought Lex as he followed Elspeth up more stairs and along a labyrinth of corridors.

'I feel as if I should be leaving a trail of breadcrumbs,' he said, and Elspeth smiled as she opened a door at last.

'It's not as complicated as it seems the first time,' she promised as she left.

Lex was dismayed to see her go. He had considered asking her to look after Freya, but that would have meant admitting that he couldn't cope, and that wasn't something Lex could do. He wasn't the kind of person who admitted failure or asked for help.

It would have been different if Elspeth had *offered* to take Freya. Then he could have legitimately handed her over. But as it was, she simply smiled and assured him that she would make sure Romy knew where they were, and Lex was left to grit his teeth and get on with it.

He found himself in a magnificent guest room, dominated by a four-poster bed, and with swagged curtains at the windows. The cot, pushchair, high chair and assorted baby bags were neatly stacked in the corner, together with his own briefcase and overnight bag, which had clearly been put in here by mistake.

It was all boding very well for the deal, he thought. If Romy, as a very junior member of the negotiating team, had been allocated a room like this, Willie Grant must be doing more than considering their offer.

Feeling more confident, Lex tried putting Freya down again, but she was having none of it. She insisted on being picked up again, and amused herself for the next few minutes by pulling at his hair, batting his nose and trying to twist his lips with surprisingly strong little fingers.

'Ouch!' Lex began to get quite ruffled. Where was Romy? It felt as if he had been walking around with Freya for hours now, but when he looked at his watch he was astounded to see that barely thirty minutes had passed since Romy had handed him her daughter and left. Surely she had to be here soon?

Worse was to come.

Wincing as he pulled her fingers from his nose, Lex was alarmed to see that Freya's face had gone bright red and screwed up with effort.

'What's the—?'

He stopped as an unmistakable smell wafted up from her nappy.

'Oh, God. Oh, no…'

Dangled abruptly at arm's length, Freya started to cry again.

'No, no, don't cry…your mother will be here soon…just hold on…'

But Freya didn't want to hold on. She was miserable and uncomfortable and missing the reassuring solidity of his body. She cried and cried until Lex, who had been pretending to himself that he didn't know what needed to be done, was driven to investigating the bag he had seen Romy take to the Ladies with Freya in the pub, what seemed like a lifetime ago.

He did know what had to be done. He just didn't want to face it.

'Where are you, Romy?' he muttered.

The bag contained fresh nappies and a pack of something called baby wipes. Lex made a face, but took the bag and the baby into the bathroom and looked around for a towel. He had a nasty feeling things were going to get messy.

Cursing fluently under his breath, he spread the towel as best he could one-handed, and laid Freya, still screaming, on top of it.

'Please stop crying,' he begged her, wrenching at his tie in dismay at the task ahead of him.

In response, Freya redoubled her cries.

'OK, OK.' Lex dragged his hands through his hair and took a deep breath. 'You can do this,' he told himself.

He rolled up his sleeves and studied the fastenings on Freya's dungarees. So far, so good. Gingerly, he pulled them off her and then, averting his face, managed to unfasten the nappy.

'Ugh.'

Grimacing horribly, he tugged the dirty nappy free, holding it out as far away from him as humanly possible, and put it in a waste-paper basket. Then he braced himself for the next stage of the process.

'God, what am I doing?' Lex muttered as he pulled off some sheets of loo paper. 'I'm Chief Executive of Gibson & Grieve. I make deals and I make money. I negotiate. I direct. I don't wipe bottoms. How did I come to this?'

And then—at last!—came the sound of the door opening. 'Lex?' Romy called.

'In here.'

When Romy crossed to the bathroom door, she saw Lex crouched on the floor, a fistful of loo paper in his hand and Freya kicking and grizzling on a towel in front of him. Both of them looked up at Romy as she appeared in the doorway, with almost identical expressions of relief.

'Oh, thank God!' said Lex in heartfelt tones. 'Where have you *been*?'

'With Willie, then I went to the kitchen to find Freya some supper.'

Romy looked from her daughter to Lex. She had never seen him less than immaculate before, but now his hair was standing on end, his tie askew and his sleeves rolled up above his wrists.

He looked so harried that she wanted to laugh, but it seemed less than tactful when he had clearly been doing his best.

'She was crying,' Lex said defensively, as if she had demanded to know what he thought he was doing. 'I thought she needed her nappy changing but I'm not really sure what I'm doing…'

Romy could only guess what *that* admission had cost him. 'It was very brave of you to have a go at all,' she told him. 'Shall I take over now?'

'She's all yours.'

Lex couldn't get up quickly enough. He watched as Romy cleaned the baby and put on a clean nappy with the minimum of fuss.

'You make it look so simple,' he said almost re-sentfully, and she glanced up at him with a smile.

'Practice,' she said.

Freya was wreathed in smiles once more. Romy lifted her up and kissed her, and the tenderness in her expression closed a fist around Lex's heart and squeezed.

Turning abruptly on his heel, he went back into the bedroom, where a plate of bread and butter with some ham and a banana was sitting on a side table. Freya's supper, presumably. Lex dreaded to imagine what she would do with that banana.

Not his problem, he reminded himself. Thank God.

'I'll leave you to it,' he called back to Romy as he retrieved his bag and briefcase. 'What time are we expected for dinner?'

Romy appeared in the doorway with Freya. 'Drinks at seven thirty.'

'Fine. I'll have time for a shower and can change these trousers.' Lex shook each leg in turn. Between Freya and the snow, he didn't think they would ever be the same again. 'I don't suppose you know which is my room?'

Romy settled Freya into the plastic chair that she had fixed to the table. She handed her the plate of bread and ham and turned to face Lex, drawing a breath.

'This one,' she said.

'All your stuff is in here,' said Lex. 'You might as well stay here, and I'll take your room.'

'This *is* our room.'

Halfway to the door, Lex stopped. Frowned as he realised what she was saying. 'You mean…?'

'I'm afraid so.' Faint colour touched Romy's cheeks. She hadn't been looking forward to breaking this to Lex. 'There seems to have been some kind of misunderstanding when Summer rang up,' she said carefully. 'They thought that because we were bringing a baby, we were all together.'

'Didn't you tell them that's not the case?'

She hesitated. 'Not yet.'

'Why on earth not?'

'I wasn't sure what to do.'

Edgily, Romy walked over to the window and pulled back the curtain. Outside, the snow was still swirling in the darkness while great, fat flakes piled up on the window sill. If they weren't careful, they would be snowed in here, and then what would happen?

Lex eyed her back in baffled frustration. 'What do you mean, you weren't sure? You could just tell the truth!'

'The thing is, Willie was so *pleased*.' Romy turned from the window, trying to make Lex understand what it had been like. 'He was supposed to be showing me some charter, but he really just wanted to talk about you, and how happy he was to discover you weren't at all like your reputation. There he was, expecting some soulless businessman, and you turn up with a baby and start bonding with his beastly dog…Willie was absolutely delighted to discover that you were a family man after all!'

'But I'm not Freya's father,' Lex objected, pacing back from the door. 'We told him that.'

'I know, but that only makes it better from his point of view. Apparently his mother was a single mother who struggled without any support from her family or his father or anyone, and helping single mothers is a big issue with him.'

Romy fiddled with her bracelets. 'He just assumed that you and I were...' Somehow she just couldn't bring herself to say 'lovers'. It was too close to the truth. And too far.

'Together,' she said in the end. 'So the fact that you're prepared to be in a relationship with me and be a hands-on father figure to Freya...well, that clinched it for Willie.'

Hands-on? Lex raked a hand through his hair. This was getting worse and worse!

'Why didn't you put him right straight away?'

'Because *you* told me you wanted this deal signed at all costs!' said Romy defensively. 'This is important, you said.'

'Good God, Romy, you can't have thought I meant you to lie to the man!'

'I didn't *lie*. I just...didn't tell him he'd got it all wrong. I could barely get a word in edgeways as it was.'

Romy was starting to get cross. 'Willie was going on and on about how pleased he was to discover that you weren't at all like your reputation, and how much happier he felt knowing that Grant's was going to be part of a chain run by a man with the right priorities. At what point was I supposed to interrupt and say that actually you weren't like that at all, and that actually you didn't want anything to do with me at all and that you'd rather stick pins in your eyes than deal with a baby?'

'There must have been something you could do!' Lex took another turn around the room, watched round-eyed by Freya, who was intrigued by his agitation. 'Eat your supper!' he said to her irritably as he went past, and obligingly she stuffed another finger of bread in her mouth.

'Leave Freya out of it!' snapped Romy, moving to stand protectively over her daughter.

Picking up the banana, she began to peel it as she made herself calm down. There was no point in getting into an argument with Lex. She didn't for a moment think he would sack her out of spite, but, when all was said and done, he was still her boss.

'Look,' she said after a moment, 'I know it seems awkward, and I'm sorry, but I just didn't know what to do. It seemed so important to Willie.'

She sliced up the banana and put it on Freya's plate, while Lex continued to prowl around the room. 'I got the sense that he'd almost decided that he didn't want to sell to you, but, between Freya and the dog, you've changed his mind. He told me in the tower that he's really keen for the deal to go ahead as soon as possible now.'

Lex sucked in his breath at the news. This was the moment he had been waiting for. He wanted to punch the air and shout *'Yes!'* but it didn't seem appropriate now that everything was muddled with this misunderstanding about his relationship with Romy.

He paced some more. He wanted this deal—oh, how he wanted it!—but did he really want it under false pretences?

Romy was watching him warily. 'I was afraid that if I told Willie the truth, he would be so disappointed that he'd change his mind back again,' she said.

'I wasn't just thinking about you,' she added as Lex pinched the bridge of his nose between finger and thumb. 'I was thinking about all the work Tim and the rest of the team have put in on this deal. We all want it as much as you do. So rather than throw up my hands in horror when I realised what Willie was thinking, I thought I should talk to you first. You're the boss,' she said. 'I think you should decide whether you tell him the truth or not.'

Lex had ended up at the window. He stood, exactly where Romy had done, looking broodingly out at the snow that spiralled silently past, catching the light from the room in a brief blur of white before drifting down into the darkness. His hands were thrust into his trouser pockets, his shoulders stiff with exasperation.

'God, what a mess!' he said with a short, humourless laugh.

Romy said nothing. It seemed to her that there was little more that she *could* say now. It was up to Lex.

Freya, quite oblivious to the tension in the room, was stuffing banana into her mouth. Romy sat down next to her and turned her bracelets while her eyes rested on the back of Lex's head. How was it that it could still look so familiar after all this time?

Unaware of her gaze, Lex tried to roll the tension from his shoulders and she sucked in a breath at the stab of memory. He was such a guarded man, such a cool and careful man, and he held himself so tautly that it was easy to forget that beneath the suit, beneath the tie and the immaculate shirt, was a man of bone and muscle, of firm flesh and sinew, a man hard and smooth and strong.

Romy remembered running her hands over those shoulders, feeling the flex of responsive muscles beneath her touch. His back was broad and solid and warm, his skin sleek and underlaid with steel.

She couldn't see his face, but she knew that it would be set in harsh lines, and that a nerve would be jumping in his jaw. She could go to him, put her arms around him from behind, and lay her cheek against his back. She could hold onto his hardness and his strength, and offer in return the comfort of her warmth and her softness. She could tell him that she would be there for him, whatever happened.

She could, but she wouldn't.

It was just a fantasy. A stupid fantasy, Romy knew. A *dangerous* fantasy.

The trouble with Lex was that he made her feel things she didn't want to feel. Something about him bypassed all her rational processes and tugged at a chord deep inside her. Romy didn't want it to be love. Love, she knew, laid you open. It made you vulnerable, made you blind. It was a trap that could spring shut at any moment, and she had no intention of blundering into it. She couldn't afford to get tangled up in loving anyone, least of all a man who had made it plain that he had no interest in Freya.

I do want you, he had said. *I just don't want a baby.*

And that wasn't a problem, because she didn't want *him*, Romy reminded herself.

So, no fantasies. No remembering, no thinking about how he had felt or the clean, male smell of his skin. She was here on business, and she had better not forget it.

The silence lengthened, broken only by Freya loudly enjoying the banana. Bath time next, Romy thought, and was about to get to her feet when Lex spoke at last.

'I went to see my father last week,' he said suddenly, without looking round.

Thrown by the apparent change of subject, Romy hesitated. 'How is he?' she asked at last.

'A stroke is a terrible thing.' Lex kept his eyes on the snow. 'He's trapped in a useless body, but his mind is as sharp as ever. He was such a powerful man, always in control, and now all he can do is lie there. He can't bear the humiliation of it.'

'He must be glad to see you,' Romy said, not entirely sure where this was going.

'Must he? I think he hates the fact that I can walk into the room on my own. He hates the fact that I can walk out. He hates the fact that I run Gibson & Grieve now. I don't know which of us dreads my visits more,' said Lex bleakly.

'But still you go.'

'My mother says he wants to know what's going on at Gibson & Grieve now he's not there any more. She says it's all that keeps him going. It's certainly all we've got to talk about.'

Lex's mouth turned down at the corners. 'You know what's the worst thing about those visits? It's that every time I hope that he'll think the company is doing all right. You'd think I'd know by now that he's never going to say, "Well done",' he added, unable to keep the bitterness from his voice. 'I could tell him we'd quadrupled our profits, and he'd still say it wasn't good enough!'

'Is that why you feel you have to prove something with this deal?'

'Damn right it is.' Lex turned to face her at last. 'When I told him about taking over Grant's, my father said that Grant wouldn't sell. He said he'd approached him before, and they couldn't make it work, so I wouldn't be able to pull it off either. Talking is a big effort for him nowadays, and his speech is slurred, but he made sure I got that message. It won't work, he said.'

Lex's jaw was clenched. 'I'm going to go back and tell him that Grant *will* sell, that it *will* work. I want him to know that he was wrong, and that Gibson & Grieve is bigger and better without him.'

CHAPTER FIVE

ROMY bit her lip. 'Lex, he's very ill. Making him admit that he was wrong won't make you feel any better.'

'It's not about *feeling*,' said Lex angrily. 'It's about doing what's best for the company. And signing this deal with Grant is the best thing for Gibson & Grieve.'

'So…?' Romy's dark eyes were wary.

'So let's not disillusion him.' Lex made up his mind so abruptly that he couldn't believe that he had been hesitating. Surely it had been obvious?

He pulled the curtain back across the window and came to join Romy and Freya at the table.

'You've told me it makes a difference to Willie if we're together or not, and if that's the case I'm not prepared to risk him changing his mind. If we start bleating on about separate rooms and not really being a couple, it'll just be embarrassing for everybody.'

'That's what I thought,' said Romy.

'What does it matter if Willie thinks we're a couple?' Lex, talking himself into the whole idea, made the mistake of looking at Freya, who smiled at him through a mouthful of banana. He averted his eyes quickly. 'It'll only be for a night. How hard can that be?'

'As long as he doesn't ask too many personal questions.' Romy thought she should inject a note of caution, but Lex was committed now.

'We're going to talk business tonight,' he said. 'If Willie is really concerned about getting the best deal for Grant's Supersavers, he'll have more important questions to ask.'

How hard could it be? Lex had asked, and at the time it had seemed all quite straightforward. The deal was within his grasp. He and Romy would have dinner with Willie Grant. They would discuss the arrangements and come to a gentleman's agreement, and the deal would be done. The next day, he and Romy would return to London. Romy would go back to Acquisitions, Freya would go to the crèche that he had had no idea existed, and he could tell his father that he had succeeded where he never could.

Simple.

Only he hadn't counted on the intimacy of

sharing a room with Romy. Lex flipped open his computer to check the markets, while Romy had a bath with Freya, but it was impossible to concentrate with the squeals and splashes and laughter coming out of the bathroom. Romy's vividly coloured outfit hung on the wardrobe door, and her perfume lingered distractingly in the air, coiling around his mind and making the Dow Jones Index dance in front of his eyes.

Worse was to come. The door opened, and Romy came out, carrying Freya. 'I found this behind the door,' she said, gesturing down at the towelling robe. 'I hope no one will mind if I use it.'

'I'm sure they won't.' Lex's voice came out as a humiliating rasp, and he cleared his throat and scowled at the screen. Much good it did him. There might as well have been a photo of Romy there instead, her skin glowing, her hair damp to her shoulders, her face alight with joy in her daughter....

Romy threw a towel on the floor and laid Freya on it. 'There's not much room in the bathroom,' she explained over her shoulder, 'so I thought it would be easier to dry her out here. It's all yours.'

Of course, what he should have done was get up straight away and have a shower, but instead Lex sat on at the computer, pretending to himself that he was working, forcing his eyes back to the screen whenever they drifted over to where Romy was kissing Freya's toes and blowing raspberries on her tummy while Freya shrieked with delighted laughter and clutched at her mother's hair.

Lex knew exactly how silky it would feel in Freya's fingers. He knew how it felt tickling his skin, and memory hit him like a blow to his diaphragm: the hitch in his chest at Romy's pliant warmth in his arms, her soft laughter in his ear, her kisses drifting down his throat, down, down, down... All at once he lost track of his breathing. It got all muddled up with the twist of his guts and the vice around his chest and he had to force his lungs back to order.

Inflate, deflate. In, out. In, out. Slow, steady.

No problem. There was no need to panic. There was plenty of oxygen.

Lex switched off the computer. There was little point in sitting there staring at nothing.

'I'll go and have a shower then.' Even to his own ears his voice sounded unfamiliar.

Romy looked up briefly. 'Good idea. I'm going to take Freya down to the kitchen and warm some milk for her.'

She wasn't bothered by the intimacy of the situation at all, Lex realised, chagrined. She was too absorbed in her baby to think about him.

To remember Paris.

To wonder about that four poster bed or where he would sleep.

Frankly, it was a relief when Romy and Freya had gone. Lex showered and shaved and reminded himself what they were doing there. This was business. The deal was what mattered, and it was almost within his grasp. This was not the time to get distracted by silky hair or bare feet or joyous laughter.

By the time Romy came back with a sleepy Freya, Lex had himself back under control. He was buttoning a dark blue shirt when she knocked lightly and opened the door.

'Don't worry, I'm decent,' he said with a sardonic look. 'Although I'm not sure there'd be much point in being shy even if I wasn't. It's not as if we haven't seen each other's bodies before.'

That was better, Lex told himself. He sounded indifferent, as if he hadn't even *noticed* that she had been naked beneath that towelling robe earlier. As if it would never occur to him to think about touching her, tasting her.

Romy had set the cot up in a corner. She laid Freya down and switched off the lamps nearby, glad of the excuse to dim the light and hide the colour staining her cheeks.

'That was a long time ago,' she reminded him uncomfortably. 'We're different people now.'

She just wished she *felt* different. It had been bad enough when Lex was sitting there at his computer, but now he was tucking his shirt into his trousers, doing up his cuffs, slinging a tie around his neck, as if they were a real couple getting ready to go out for the evening.

But if they were a real couple, she could go over to Lex and slide her arms around his waist. She could kiss his newly shaved jaw and run her fingers through his damp hair.

She could tug the shirt out of his trousers once more and slide her hands over his bare chest.

Make him smile, feel his arms close around her.

Whisper that there was time before they had to leave. Time to hold each other. Time to touch. Time to make love.

Romy swallowed hard. There was no time now. That time was past.

'I'd better change.'

Wincing at the huskiness in her voice, she took her outfit into the bathroom. She saw immediately that Lex had tidied up. The bath mat had been hung up, the towels neatly folded and drying on the rail. The top was back on the shampoo and the toothbrushes were standing to attention in a glass.

Romy sighed. She would have tidied the bathroom herself if he had left it. Growing up, she had often heard Phin mock Lex for his nit-picking ways, and the chief executive's insistence on precision and neatness was something of a joke in the office, but it didn't seem quite so funny now. It just underlined the fact that a man with Lex's obsessive need for order would never be able to cope with the chaos of living with children.

And why would that be a problem? Romy asked her reflection.

It wouldn't, because Lex would never have to live with a child. He would never want to. Tonight was the closest he would get to family life, and Romy was quite sure it would be enough for him.

And that wasn't a problem for her, either.

Was it?

Freya was asleep. Romy left one of the bedside lamps on and closed the door softly behind her. 'Let's go,' she said.

They made their way back to the library together. 'This place is enormous,' said Lex as they turned the corner to find themselves in yet another picture-lined corridor. 'Why does Willie stay here on his own?'

'Duncardie reminds him of his wife. She loved it here, apparently, so don't go telling him he'd be better off back in the city.'

'I'm not completely insensitive,' Lex said huffily.

He was hummingly aware of Romy next to him.

She had emerged from the bathroom wearing silk trousers and a camisole, with some kind of loose silk jacket. Lex wasn't very good on fashion, but the colours and the print made him think of heat and spices and coconut palms swaying in the breeze.

He could hear the faint swish of the slippery fabric as she walked, could picture it slithering over her skin, and he swallowed painfully. Her hair was piled up in a way that managed to look elegant and messy at the same time, and, with her bracelets and dangly earrings, she came across as vivid, interesting, and all too touchable. Next to her, Lex knew, he seemed stiff and conventional in his suit.

Willie was waiting for them in the library. He was standing in front of the fire, Magnus at his feet, and in an expansive mood. 'We'll talk details over dinner,' he said when he had welcomed them in and complimented Romy on her outfit, 'but I'm happy to agree in principle to a merger of Grant's Supersavers with Gibson & Grieve.'

'Oh, that's wonderful news!' Getting into her role, Romy smiled and hugged Lex, whose arm went round her quite instinctively.

She was warm and soft and slender, and his hand rested on the curve of her hip. He breathed in the scent of her hair and felt silk slip a little under his palm, a sharp, erotic shock that made his heart clench.

Head reeling, incapable of saying anything, Lex gave himself up to the pleasure of holding her for the first time in twelve years, until Romy widened her eyes meaningfully at him. 'Isn't it, darling?' she prompted him as she disengaged herself.

'Wonderful,' he managed.

It was barely more than a croak, but Willie wouldn't notice. He was too busy being kissed by Romy. It was Willie's turn to have that smooth cheek against his own, to feel that vibrant warmth pressed against him. To be enveloped in her glow.

Lex wanted to kill him.

Now Willie was returning Romy's hug. Patting her shoulder. Smiling at her. Good God, why didn't he stick a tongue down her throat and be done with it? Lex thought savagely, just as Willie looked over Romy's shoulder. The expression on Lex's face made the shaggy white brows lift in surprise, and then amused understanding.

'I think we should celebrate, don't you?' he said as he let Romy go.

The deal of his career, and Lex had never felt less like celebrating. What was the matter with him? he thought, appalled at his own behaviour. This was the moment he had been waiting for, the deal within his grasp at last, and all he could do was think about how smooth and warm Romy's skin would be beneath that silk top.

He rearranged his face into a stiff smile. 'Excellent.'

'I've got something really special to mark the occasion.' Willie beamed at them both.

'Champagne?'

'Oh, much more special than that,' he promised, turning away to a tray behind him. Reverently, he poured what looked like rich liquid gold into plain crystal tumblers.

Romy buried her nose in the glass when he handed one to her. 'Whisky,' she said, surprised, and Willie tutted as he passed a glass to Lex.

'This is no ordinary whisky. This is a fifty year old single malt. A thousand pounds a bottle,' he added just as Romy took her first sip.

'What?'

She choked, coughing and spluttering while Lex patted her on the back. Well, what else could he do? Lex asked himself. He was supposed to be a concerned lover. Of course he would pat her on the back. It wasn't just an excuse to touch her.

He was just playing his part. He wasn't thinking about how little fabric there was between his hand and her skin or how easy it would be to let the jacket slither off her shoulders. He wasn't thinking about how inviting the nape of her neck looked. How easy it would be to press his lips to it. To pull the clips from her hair and let it tumble down.

Without his being aware of it, his patting had turned into a slow rub. Romy, her eyes still watering, moved unobtrusively out of his reach.

'Thanks,' she managed, and Lex's hand fell to his side where it hung, feeling hot and heavy and uncomfortable. Not sure what to do with it now, Lex stroked Magnus's head instead.

'Better?' Willie smiled and lifted his glass when she nodded. 'In that case…*Slainthe!*'

'*Slainthe!*' echoed Lex and took a sip.

'Well?' Willie eyed him expectantly. 'What do you think?'

'Unforgettable.'

It was true. Lex was gripped by a strange sense of unreality, shot through with an intense immediacy, as if he had shifted into a parallel universe where all his senses were on high alert. He was would never forget anything about this evening: the castle in the snow, the great dog beside him, the taste of this extraordinary whisky on his tongue.

The deal of his life.

And Romy, in the firelight.

Pleased with his response, Willie waved them to the leather sofa where they had sat before. 'Sit down and tell me all about yourselves,' he invited. Or perhaps it was a command.

So much for him not asking personal questions. Romy couldn't resist a glance at Lex, who ran a finger around his collar and didn't quite meet her eye.

'What would you like to know?' he asked Willie stiffly after a moment.

'Call me a nosy old man, but I like to know who I'm doing business with,' said Willie, settling himself comfortably into his chair. 'I'm interested in how somebody with your reputation turns out be so different when you meet him face to face. I was expecting a soulless businessman, and I get a man capable of building a relationship with a beautiful woman, her baby and even my dog!'

His bright blue eyes fixed on Lex's face. 'Why do you keep Romy here a secret? I was so proud of Moira, I used to show her off whenever I could, so that everyone could see what a lucky man I was.'

Romy saw Lex's jaw clench with frustrated irritation and she slid over the sofa and put her hand on his taut thigh before he could snap back that it was none of Willie's business. Willie might have said that the deal would go ahead, but it wasn't signed yet.

'That's not Lex's fault,' she said quickly. 'I'm the one who wants to keep things a secret for now. It still feels very…new.'

That was true enough, Romy thought. By her reckoning they had been a 'couple' for all of two hours.

'Lex is technically my boss,' she went on. 'I didn't want my colleagues to think that I'd got the job because of him. I want to prove myself first.'

Willie chuckled. 'So all this time we've been talking about the deal, you've known more about Lex than anyone?'

Also probably true. Faint colour tinged Romy's cheeks.

'We don't normally work together,' she said. 'It's just that Tim couldn't come, and I couldn't leave Freya…so we all came together.'

'And I'm glad you did,' said Willie. 'I'm surprised to hear that this is a new thing. I got the impression that you've known each other a long time somehow.'

'We have.' To Romy's relief, Lex managed to unlock his jaw, and she took her hand from his thigh before it started feeling too comfortable there. 'Our mothers have been friends since they were at school,' he said. 'I've known Romy since she was born.'

That went down very well with Willie. 'Ah… childhood sweethearts? Just like Moira and I.'

'I wouldn't say that exactly, would you, Lex?' Romy decided it was better to stick to the truth as far as possible, or they would get hopelessly muddled. 'Lex was older,' she confided to Willie. 'The truth is, he was hardly aware I existed before I was eighteen!'

'Of course I knew you existed,' said Lex with a touch of irritation, and he yanked at his tie as if it felt too tight. He looked cross and more than a little ruffled, Romy thought. Not at all like a man who was madly in love with her.

Funny, that.

She plastered on an adoring smile and leaned into his shoulder. Winsome wasn't a look she did well, but it looked as if she was going to have to do the work for both of them.

'It's not as if it was love at first sight, though,' she pointed out.

'It felt like it.'

Much to Romy's surprise, Lex appeared to have come to the same conclusion, or at least to have realised that he wasn't giving a very good impression of a man who had found the love of his life.

'I hadn't seen Romy for three or four years.' He turned to tell Willie the story. 'You know what it's like when you first leave home. I'd lost track of family occasions once I was at university. I remembered a gangly, unruly girl of fourteen or so, but then I called in to see my parents one weekend and Romy was there, and suddenly she was all grown up.'

And then before Romy realised quite what he was doing, he had taken her hand. His fingers closed around hers, warm and strong, and her heart began to bump against her ribs. She remembered that day so well.

'I just stood and stared,' Lex said, looking into Romy's eyes, and it was almost as if he had forgotten Willie entirely. 'Until then, I thought falling in love was just an expression,' he said, his voice very deep. 'But falling was just how it felt.'

He could still remember that moment, the lurch of his heart, the tumbling sensation as if he had slipped over the side of a cliff, the terror and exhilaration of falling, falling, out of control.

The pain of crashing into reality.

Lex took a gulp of his whisky. It burned down his throat, steadied him. Maybe thousand-pound bottles of whisky would have helped twelve years ago. Belatedly realising that he was still holding Romy's hand, he let it go.

'Eighteen?' Willie was evidently doing some calculations in his head. 'You've been together a long time, then.'

Romy glanced at Lex, and then away. 'No. That time, the first time, we just had a week. We ran off to Paris together. It was very romantic. We had the most…' She made a helpless gesture, unable to describe to Willie what that week had been like. 'It was like stumbling into a different world, but we both knew then it couldn't last.'

'I thought it could,' Lex contradicted her. 'I asked her to marry me,' he told Willie, 'and she said no.'

'I was only eighteen!' Romy cried. 'I was much too young to think about getting married. You agreed that it would have been crazy—'

She stopped, realising that Lex had agreed that morning. He hadn't thought it was a crazy idea in Paris. But this wasn't something they should be discussing in front of Willie. They were supposed to be in love, not two people still wrangling about the past.

She pinned on a smile. 'Anyway, the upshot was that we went our separate ways,' she told Willie. 'I stayed in France for that year, and then I came home to go to university, but when I graduated I still had itchy feet. I spent the next few years working my way around the world. I ended up in Indonesia.'

Sensing Lex growing restless, Romy decided to speed the story up a bit. 'That's where I got pregnant. I came home to have the baby, but I didn't see Lex again until his brother's wedding last summer.'

No need to tell Willie that Lex hadn't come near her all day.

'Meanwhile, I'd been at Gibson & Grieve, doing what I'd always done,' said Lex. 'Then last summer, Phin got married, and Romy was there…'

'And you fell in love with her all over again?'

Lex drew a breath, then let it out slowly. 'Yes,' he said.

When he looked at Romy, her eyes were dark and wary. 'Yes,' he said again. 'I'd never forgotten her—how could I? I think I'd spent all those years just waiting for her to come home. I'd try going out with other women, but none of them made me feel the way Romy did. I was Phin's best man. I remember standing by his side, and turning to watch the bride, and seeing Romy sitting a few pews behind.'

Willie seemed to be enjoying the story. 'And that was that?'

'That was that,' agreed Lex.

There was a pause. Romy couldn't believe how convincing he sounded. Beside him on the sofa, she studied him under her lashes. He was so lean and solid and restrained in his suit. What must it be costing him to come out with all this rubbish about being in love with her still? Only that morning, on the plane, he had reminded her that any feelings he'd once had were long dead.

We've both moved on, he had said.

He was a much better actor than she had expected him to be. Romy was sure he must be hating the need to pretend, to talk about *feelings*, but then, he had an incentive. He would do whatever it took to get Willie's agreement.

'Well, you've done a good job of keeping all this a secret,' Willie was saying admiringly. 'I've been trying to find out everything I can about you and there's been no hint of it. I don't mind telling you, it made all the difference to me that you were happy to get involved with a baby as well as Romy,' he said to Lex. 'That told me that you're a man I can trust with Grant's Supersavers, that you're a man who understands what's really important in life.'

'I do,' said Lex. He smiled at Romy, who did her best to conceal her amazement at how wholeheartedly he was entering into the pretence, and took her hand once more. 'I thought I'd never find her again, and now that I have, I'm not going to let her go again. Freya's part of the package.'

Romy's eyes widened as he lifted her hand and kissed her knuckles. 'I've waited a long time for Romy to agree to marry me, and now she has. Between that and a deal to secure Grant's Supersavers, I've got everything I ever wanted.'

Willie was delighted. 'That deserves another toast!'

He hauled himself out of his chair to find the malt, thus missing the look Romy was giving Lex, who looked blandly back at her. She tried to tug her hand away, but he kept a firm hold of it as Willie splashed more of the precious whisky into their glasses.

'Congratulations,' said Willie, lifting his glass towards them both. 'Here's to love lost and found!'

'Here's to love,' Lex and Romy agreed, smiling hard, but not meeting each other's eyes.

'What on earth did you say that for?' Romy demanded as the bedroom door closed behind them at the end of that memorable evening.

'Say what?' said Lex, tugging his tie loose.

'You know what! About getting married!'

Romy would have liked to have shouted, but Freya was asleep in the corner, so she was restricted to a furious whisper, which didn't improve her temper.

Lex just shrugged and pulled the tie from his neck, undoing the top button of his shirt with a sigh of relief. 'If we're going to pretend, we might as well do it properly. And you've got to admit, it did the trick. Willie was delighted.'

'He was delighted before. You didn't need to complicate it with marriage.' Romy sat on the edge of the bed and kicked off her shoes bad-temperedly.

'People of that generation feel more comfortable with marriage. How else could I convince him that I was going to do right by you and Freya?'

'Everyone knows that I'm never going to get married,' she said, unable to explain just how uneasy the very idea made her.

'People change.'

'Not me!'

'No,' Lex agreed with a sardonic look, 'I know not you. Fortunately, Willie doesn't have any idea how stubborn you are.'

'It's not about stubbornness,' said Romy.

'Isn't it?'

'No. It's about being realistic, not stubborn.'

Lex shook his head. 'No, it's not. It's about being afraid. You're afraid of marriage because you think it might end up badly like your parents' marriage did, and you'll be hurt again. Fair enough. I understand that. But I don't quite see what the problem is here. We're not getting married. It's just a pretence.'

'I know.' Romy sighed, and twisted her bracelets fretfully. 'I know you're right. I just wish Willie wasn't quite so thrilled. I don't like lying to him.'

'It's a bit late to worry about that now,' said Lex, exasperated. 'This was all your idea in the first place!' His voice had risen, until Romy pointed at Freya's cot and laid a finger over her lips. 'And you were the one who started on the "darlings",' he added more quietly.

'I thought it would make us look more convincing,' she said. 'Little did I know that, once you got going, you would turn in an Oscar-winning performance! You nearly had *me* convinced!'

'Look, what's the problem?' Lex had started on his buttons now. 'We've done it. Willie's agreed to the sale.'

As promised, they had discussed it over an excellent dinner, and come to what Willie called a 'gentleman's agreement'. The lawyers would draw up a detailed contract. He and Willie would sign it and the deal would be done.

'We've done exactly what we set out to do,' he reminded Romy. 'We can go home tomorrow, and no one else will ever know that you once pretended for five seconds that you would consider the possibility of marriage.'

Romy wished he would stop unbuttoning his shirt. It was distracting her. Averting her eyes, she began to pull off her bangles one by one.

'What if Willie finds out that we're not really engaged?'

'You said yourself he never leaves Duncardie now,' Lex pointed out. 'And we've already told him why we're keeping it a secret for now.'

'I suppose so.'

Romy wasn't sure why the whole question had made her so twitchy. It was something to do with sitting next to Lex all evening. With the feel of his fingers warm around hers, his palm strong and steady on her back, his thigh beneath her hand.

She had been desperately aware of him. Ever

since she had walked into the bathroom and seen him looking harassed at the prospect of changing Freya's nappy there had been a persistent thumping low in her belly. A jittery, fluttery, frantic feeling just beneath her skin that was part nervousness, part excitement.

How was it possible to be furious with someone and still want to wrap yourself round him? To kiss your way along his jaw and press against the lovely lean hardness of his body?

At least the argument about the stupid marriage thing had got them over the awkwardness of being alone. Having divested herself of bracelets and earrings, Romy stomped into the bathroom to get undressed. Lex might be happy to start stripping off in front of her, but she didn't have his cool.

She didn't possess a nightdress. She hadn't been expecting to share a room, so all she had with her was an old sarong. Romy eyed it dubiously as she wrapped it tightly under her arms. It was hardly the most seductive of garments, but she couldn't help wishing it were a little more substantial.

If she had had time to think about her packing, she might have considered that a castle in the Highlands in the middle of winter might not be the most appropriate place for a sarong, and then she would have been prepared with a sensible winceyette nightie that would have kept her warm and, more importantly under the current circumstances, covered. Not that Lex had shown any sign of preparing to pounce, but, still, it was unnerving to contemplate the prospect of sharing a bed with nothing but a skimpy strip of material for modesty.

Well, it would just have to do.

When Romy went back into the bedroom, holding her clothes protectively in front of her, Lex was peering in the wardrobe. He had stripped off his shirt, but still wore his trousers, to her relief. The sight of his broad, bare, smooth back was enough to dry her mouth and set her heart thudding against her ribs as it was. God only knew what state she'd be in if he'd taken off any more clothes!

'What are you doing?'

'Looking for an extra blanket,' he said without turning round. 'I'll sleep on the floor.'

'Lex, it's snowing outside! You'll freeze to death, even on the carpet.' Romy dumped her clothes on top of her overnight case and checked that Freya was still sound asleep. Having been stomach-twistingly anxious about the prospect of sleeping with him, she was now perversely determined to prove to Lex that it didn't bother her at all.

'It's an absolutely huge bed—and it's not as if we've never shared a bed before, is it?'

'No,' he said, turning to face her, 'but as you

said before, that was twelve years ago and we're different people now.'

'We're twelve years older and twelve years more grown up,' said Romy firmly, hoping to convince herself as much as Lex. 'We've got over all that.' She saw Lex's brows rise and flushed. 'You know what I mean. And even if we hadn't, how could I possibly sleep knowing that you were on the floor? There's room for ten in there,' she said, gesturing at the bed.

An exaggeration, perhaps, but it was certainly a very large bed. They would easily be able to avoid rolling into each other.

She hoped.

CHAPTER SIX

PULLING back the heavy cover, Romy climbed up into the bed and made a big show of making herself comfortable. 'It's up to you, of course,' she said, 'but if you're worried about me making a fuss about sharing a bed, then don't. I really don't see why it needs to be a big deal.'

'Well, if you're sure…'

Lex splashed water over his face and brushed his teeth. He knew Romy was right. It was only sensible. The floor would be uncomfortable, not to mention cold, and there was no convenient sofa.

She clearly wasn't bothered at the prospect, so he could hardly say that it bothered *him*. Romy might think that there was room for ten in the bed, but Lex was pretty sure that it wouldn't feel like that when he was lying beside her. It wouldn't take much to roll over and find himself next to her, and then what would happen? How would he be able to stop himself reaching for her?

No big deal, she thought.

Hah.

But there was nothing for it.

He didn't even have any pyjamas with him. Normally he slept in the buff and he hadn't expected tonight to be any different. He would definitely have to keep boxers on, Lex realised. It was going to be difficult enough without adding naked bodies into the equation, and he didn't care what Romy said about being twelve years older. Some things didn't change that much.

Remembering how cool Romy had been about the whole business, Lex took his time folding his trousers and hanging them up before he crossed over to bed. To his relief Romy had snuggled down under the cover so that only her nose and eyes were showing. That was good. It meant he couldn't see her bare shoulders, or her bare arms, or her bare legs.

But he knew they were there. Oh, yes.

The dark eyes watched with a certain wariness as he pulled back the cover on his side of the bed, switched off the light and lay down.

They weren't touching at all, but Lex was aware of her with every fibre of his being. His right side was tingling with her nearness. It would take so little to touch her.

Big enough for ten people? Lex didn't think so.

He stared up at the canopy through the dark. He should be jubilant. The deal was done. Willie Grant had agreed to sell and Gibson & Grieve would have the foothold in Scotland they had wanted for so long. He could go back to his father and show him what he had been able to do. He had everything he'd wanted.

But all he could think about was Romy, lying beside him in the darkness. He'd been aware of her all evening, and it had been a struggle to concentrate on the conversation when his mind kept swooping between memories and noticing the pure line of her throat, how her hair gleamed in the candlelight. Her face had been bright as she leaned across the table to talk to Willie, and her earrings had swung whenever she threw back her head and laughed.

Lex's throat had been so tight it was an effort to talk.

Twelve years, he had been trying to forget.

Her hair, dark and silky. The way it had swung forward as she leant over him, how soft it had felt twined around his fingers. Breathing in the scent of it as he lay with his face pressed into it, how it had made him think of long summer evenings.

Her eyes, those luminous eyes, so dark and rich and warm that brown was laughably inadequate to describe their colour. Looking into them was like falling into a different world, where nothing mattered but the feel of her, the taste of her, the need that squeezed his heart and left him dizzy and breathless.

Her mouth, too wide, too sweet. The way she turned her head and smiled sometimes.

The quicksilver feel of her, warm and vibrant and elusive. The harder he'd held onto her, the faster she'd slipped away.

The swell of his heart, the feel of it beating, when she lay quietly in his arms.

The aching emptiness when she had gone.

And now she was lying only inches away. It was a wide bed, as she had said, but it wouldn't take much to slide across the gap between them. If he rolled over, if she did, they could meet.

But Romy wasn't moving. Lex was fairly sure that she wasn't sleeping either. She was too still, her breathing too shallow.

She wasn't going to roll over, and neither was he. It was the last thing he should do, Lex knew. It had taken him a long time to gather up the wild emotions that had been flailing around inside him, but at last he had managed to press them together into a tight lump that had been settled, cold and hard, in the pit of his belly ever since. He couldn't risk dislodging it and letting all that feeling loose again.

Besides, Romy had made it very clear that she

wasn't interested in resuming a relationship—look at the fuss she had made about even pretending to be engaged!—and, even if she had been, he didn't have room in his life for a lover, let alone a baby. It was too late for that now.

Twelve years too late.

There was a muffled quality to the atmosphere when Romy woke the next morning, a strangeness about the light that was filtering through the heavy curtains on her right.

At first, puzzled by the musty fabric above her, she wondered if she was still dreaming, but a moment later memories from the day before came skidding and sliding in a rush through her mind.

Freya, sucking Lex's shoelace.

The long drive through the snow.

Willie Grant's monstrous dog.

Lex's hand on her spine.

Lex. The sag of the bed as he climbed in beside her. Knowing that he was there, near enough for her to simply reach over and…

Romy jerked upright, realising belatedly that she was alone in the four-poster. From the cot in the corner came a cooing. Freya, it seemed, was also awake, but where was Lex?

The thought had barely crossed her mind before the door was shouldered open and Lex came in carrying two mugs. He was looking positively relaxed in his suit trousers with a shirt open at the collar and the sleeves rolled above his wrists, but he still managed to exude a forcefulness that seemed to suck some of the oxygen out of the room, and Romy found herself sucking in a breath.

'Good morning,' she said, feeling ridiculously shy.

'Good morning.' Lex offered her one of the mugs. 'There doesn't seem to be anyone around, so I helped myself to some tea. I thought you might like some.'

'Thank you.' Romy pulled herself further up the pillows and took a sip of the tea. It was black and sweet, just as she liked it. She lifted her eyes to Lex. 'You remember how I take my tea!'

His gaze slid away from hers. 'I've got a good memory.'

Romy wished her own memory weren't quite so good. It might have made it easier to lie next to him all night.

But now it was morning, and Freya was singing happily to herself. Romy threw off the cover, only just remembering to secure her sarong in time, and went over to the cot.

'Hello, my gorgeous girl. How are you this morning?'

It was impossible to feel awkward or cross or

anything but joyful when Freya smiled like that. Romy picked her up and cuddled her, loving her warm, sweet smell and compact body, and Freya bumped her head into her mother's neck and grabbed fistfuls of her hair as she babbled with pleasure.

Lex looked away from their glowing faces. 'How did you sleep?' he asked after a moment.

'Fine,' said Romy, and then wondered why she was lying. 'Actually, if I hadn't just woken up, I could have sworn I didn't sleep a wink,' she confessed.

She had been too conscious of Lex, of the lean, muscled length of his body on the other side of the bed.

After so long, it had been hard to believe that he was actually there, close enough to touch, but utterly untouchable. How many times over those years had she found herself remembering that week? Remembering the feel of his body, how solid and safe he had felt, remembering how sure his hands had been, how warm his mouth, marvelling at the passion he kept bottled up beneath the austere surface.

'I didn't sleep much either,' Lex admitted.

'Looks like we'll both have to catch up tonight,' said Romy lightly.

'I've got a nasty feeling we'll be spending

another night here.' He pulled back the curtains. 'It's stopped snowing, but I doubt we'll be going anywhere today.'

She looked at him in dismay. 'We're snowed in?'

'I'm afraid so.'

Carrying Freya, Romy went to join him by the window, and caught her breath at the scene.

Outside, it was a monochrome world. Bare black trees, rimed in white. A black loch. Over everything else, a blanket of white that blurred the features of the landscape, so that it all looked oddly blank and two dimensional. Above that, a sky washed of colour, except for the faintest hint of pink staining the horizon. It was going to be a beautiful day.

But not for travelling. There were no roads visible, not even a track.

'Ah,' said Romy.

'Quite.' Lex's voice was as crisp as the snow piled high on the window sill.

Romy took Freya over to the bed and let her clamber around on the pillows while she drank her tea. 'What shall we do?'

'There's not much we *can* do. It looks as if we're stuck.' He looked at his watch. 'Summer should be in the office soon. I'll ring her in a few minutes. She'll have to reschedule tomorrow's appointments, and she can let Acquisitions know why you're not in.'

'And meanwhile, we'll have to be engaged another day?' said Romy, who thought there were more important issues to be dealt with than Lex's meetings.

'Yes,' said Lex after a beat. 'One more day. Do you think you can manage that?'

She looked back at him over the rim of her mug, her eyes dark and cautious. 'I'll have to, won't I?'

Lex fully intended to spend the day working as normal. He had the technology. Between his iPhone and his laptop, there was plenty he could do. But breakfast turned into an extended affair, with Romy chatting easily to Willie while Freya ate porridge with her fingers, and then, when Freya had a nap, Romy was determined to go outside and enjoy the snow.

'There's masses of old boots and coats in the utility room,' said Willie when Lex pointed out that she had nothing suitable to wear. 'Help yourself.'

Lex thought he might slope off to a quiet room and get on with some work then, but Romy was unimpressed. 'You're supposed to be madly in love with me,' she said when he suggested it. 'What's Willie going to think if you let me wander off into the snow on my own while you huddle over your laptop?'

Which was how Lex came to be wearing a pair

of old wellies and a faded oilskin jacket over a jumper he'd borrowed from Willie, who'd raised his brows when Lex had appeared at breakfast in a suit and tie.

Romy had never seen him in anything so shabby before, and she laughed that deep, husky laugh of hers at his expression. She was swathed in a similar jacket that had to be about six sizes too big for her, and the boots were nearly as big. A woolly hat was pulled down over her ears and a scarlet scarf wrapped jauntily around her throat. Her eyes were dark and bright. She looked, Lex thought, rather like a robin.

'I don't know what you think we're going to do out there,' he said grouchily as he pulled on a pair of gloves. 'The snow's far too deep to walk anywhere.'

'It'll be fun,' said Romy, opening the door to a glittering world. 'Just look how beautiful it is!'

Lex had been right about the snow making walking difficult. It came almost up to Romy's knees, but she refused to give up and insisted on trudging down to the lochside.

It was so cold that her teeth ached with every breath, but she was conscious of exhilaration bubbling along her veins. The light was dazzling. Every twig, every leaf bending under the weight of a pristine mound of snow, seemed to jump out at her, and when they turned to look back at Duncardie it rose out of the snow like something out of a fairy tale, with its battlements and turrets and the backdrop of the mountains.

'It looks like a stage set, doesn't it?' said Romy. 'You could almost believe a princess was sleeping in one of those towers. Perhaps we've stumbled into a magical kingdom without realising it!' She sniffed happily at the crystalline air. 'There's something unreal about today.'

'That would certainly explain why we're freezing our butts off out here when we could be warm and dry inside,' said Lex, slapping the arms of his waxed jacket for warmth.

'Come on, Lex, you've got to admit it's beautiful.' Romy turned and headed along the edge of the loch. It was hard going. She had to lift her feet high and stamp down through the snow, and she was soon puffing, but at least the exercise kept her warm.

'It looked beautiful from inside,' Lex grumbled, but he fell into step beside her.

'Look, there's Willie,' Romy said, spotting the portly figure watching them from one of the windows. She waved, and Willie waved back.

'I notice *he's* staying tucked up nice and warm. He's got more sense. Probably there shaking his head at crazy Sassenachs. '

Romy rolled her eyes and pushed him. 'Oh,

stop being such a crosspatch! I know you hate
being unlashed from the office, but it'll do you
good to get outside like this. You're getting some
exercise, breathing in all this clean air…'

'Getting frostbite,' Lex put in.

'Can you put a hand on your heart and tell me
that no part of you finds this exciting?'

Lex stopped and, surprised, she stopped too.
She was smiling. Her skin glowed, and her eyes
were brilliant. The light was so crisp that he could
see her in heart-stopping detail—the few strands
of hair escaping from beneath the hat, her brows,
the crooked front tooth—and he felt something
shift and crumple inside him.

He hoped it wasn't his heart.

He opened his mouth to answer. Afterwards,
Lex often wondered what he would have said,
and if it would have been the truth, but before he
could decide Romy caught sight of something
behind him and terror rinsed the smile from her
face. Sucking in a sharp breath, she stumbled
towards him, grabbed him by the waist and buried
her head in his chest.

Instinctively, Lex closed his arms around her,
and looked over his shoulder. Magnus, the Irish
wolfhound, was bounding towards them, snapping
at the snow with his great jaws. His muzzle was
encrusted with white and as he got close he barked

with exuberance and shook joyously, spraying snow everywhere.

Romy made a tiny sound deep in her throat and burrowed closer, as if she were trying to get inside his jacket.

'He's playing,' said Lex calmly. 'He won't hurt you.' Then, to the dog, 'Magnus, *sit*!'

Surprised at the sudden command, Magnus skidded to a halt and sat, tongue lolling.

'Let him sniff your hand.'

In response, Romy held tighter, but Lex was stronger and had already taken her hand in its glove and was stretching it towards the dog, who sniffed curiously.

'Now stroke his head.'

'I can't,' muttered Romy, shrinking as far from the dog as she could get without letting go of Lex.

'You can.' Lex moved her hand to the wiry head. Heart pounding, Romy let her glove rest there for a second before she whipped it back.

Lex clicked his tongue. 'That's not a stroke. Do it again.'

'He'll bite me.'

'Romy, look into his eyes.'

Romy was stuck. She didn't dare let go of Lex and walk away past the dog, but if she stayed where she was she would have to touch the dog again.

Resentfully, she turned her head against Lex's

chest and made herself look into the dog's eyes. They weren't a rabid red, as she had imagined, but a warm, liquid brown and their expression, she realised once she had got past the dog's monstrous size and those fearsome teeth, was calm and alert and not in the least aggressive.

Very, very cautiously, Romy let go of Lex and laid her hand on the dog's head once more. Her heart jerked as Magnus butted his nose upwards, and she would have snatched her hand away if she hadn't been afraid that Lex would think her a coward or, worse, make her stroke him again.

'See?' said Lex. 'He likes that.'

And Magnus didn't bite her hand off. He just sat there, watching her with intelligent brown eyes as she patted him. Romy let out a shaky breath. She was stroking a dog! She felt quite giddy with it.

'Well done,' said Lex, and added to the dog, 'Good dog. Go on, off you go now.'

With that, Magnus took off, scattering snow as he went.

Romy laughed unsteadily. 'I can't believe it! I stroked that huge dog!' She watched him running in wide, exuberant circles, a faint, puzzled frown between her brows. 'I feel...liberated,' she realised after a moment.

'That's because you confronted your fear,' said Lex. 'It's a hard thing to do.'

'I bet *you've* never had to do it.'

Romy set off again through the snow. She was remembering how she had clutched at him and wincing inwardly. For someone so determined to look after herself, it had only taken the sight of a big dog for her to throw herself into Lex's arms, acting entirely on instinct. And the worst thing was how *safe* she had felt there. It wasn't a comfortable thought.

'I can't imagine you ever being afraid of anything,' she said.

There was a tiny pause. When she glanced at Lex, she found him watching her, but as their eyes met he looked away. 'You'd be surprised,' he said.

'What are *you* afraid of?' she asked, her expression rife with disbelief, but he shook his head.

'I'm too scared to tell you.'

Romy laughed. She was suddenly very happy. She wasn't sure if it was the snow, creaking and squeaking beneath their boots, the sunshine or the purity of the air.

Or the man beside her.

When she glanced at him under her lashes, his austere profile was etched in startling detail against the sky. She could see the texture of his skin, every hair in the dark brows, the touch of grey at his temples that made her feel oddly wistful. He had a big nose that suited his strong face, and something about the line of his jaw made Romy ache with longing and memory.

She could remember how it felt to trail her lips along that jaw. She remembered the smell of him, the taste of him, the roughness of his skin where a faint stubble pricked.

She wanted to do it again. Lex was so big, so solid. She wanted to throw her arms about him and hold onto all that hardness and all that strength, not because she was scared of the dog, but because she could.

Which was pathetic, she knew. And wrong. Because she didn't need anyone else to be strong. She could be strong on her own. She had to be.

Anyway, it wasn't his strength that appealed, Romy told herself as that sudden wash of happiness was sucked away like a wave and something darker and more primitive crashed through her in its place.

Lust, plain and simple. She wanted to run her hands over him and press her mouth to his throat. She wanted to push her fingers through his thick hair and lick his skin. To taste him, touch him, kiss his lashes, his mouth, his *mouth*, and, oh, God, in spite of the cold, Romy could feel heat flooding her, burning in her cheeks and pooling deep inside her.

Desperate to distract herself, she bent and grabbed a handful of snow. Packing it into a ball, she threw it at Lex, who was stamping along beside her, absorbed in his own thoughts. The snowball glanced off his arm, and he turned, startled to see Romy eyeing him with a mixture of guilt and wariness as she stooped to try again.

Something flared in Lex's pale eyes. 'Right, you asked for it!' he said, scooping up his own snowball. His aim was much better than Romy's and, although she turned quickly away, it hit her right on her hat.

Her attempt missed him completely, of course, but she was already backing away, laughing as she tried to collect more ammunition. Lex's next snowball caught her on the shoulder and she fell back For the next few minutes, they hurled snow at each other like a couple of kids, until Romy stumbled in the deep snow. She would have fallen if Lex hadn't grabbed her arm and held her up with one hand. In his other, he held a huge snowball that he lifted, ready to stuff it down her neck.

'No, no, please!' Romy was laughing and shrieking at the same time. She was covered in snow by then, but the thought of it down her neck… Ugh! She couldn't remember the last time she'd had so much fun.

'Do you give in?'

'I give in ! I give in! You win!'

'All right, then.' Lex let the snowball fall, but he didn't let go of her arm. They had both been laughing, but all at once their smiles faded and their eyes locked with an almost audible click as the glittering landscape shrank to a bubble where there were just the two of them, staring at each other.

'Do you think Willie is still watching?' he asked softly.

'I…don't know,' said Romy with difficulty.

'If we were really engaged, I'd probably kiss you now, wouldn't I?'

'You might.' Romy's throat was so tight, it came out as an embarrassing squeak.

'And would you kiss me back? If we were really engaged?'

'Probably,' she managed.

Lex brought his gloved hands up to cup her face, and Romy trembled with a terrible anticipation.

'Then let's show Willie just how in love we are,' he said, and bent his mouth to hers.

His lips were warm, so warm in contrast to the stinging cold of the air, and so sure. They sent Romy plummeting through twelve long years, and she clutched at Lex's jacket, gripped by a dizzying mixture of excitement and fear and utter peace. Her senses whirled as she swung wildly between extremes, between heat and cold, between then and now. Between stillness and rush. Between the sense of coming home and the sense of standing on the edge of a dizzying drop.

When Lex pulled her closer and deepened the kiss, Romy wrapped her arms around him and kissed him back harder, breathless at the rightness of it. It felt so good to taste him again, to hold him again. Every cell in her body was sighing—no, was singing—'At last! At *last*!' The sunlight glinting on the snow was inside her, sparkling and flickering and shimmering along her veins in a glittery rush.

They broke for breath, kissed again before they could realise just what they were doing. Or that was how it felt to Romy, who had abandoned any attempt to think and was desperate to hold onto this moment, pressed against Lex's hard body, kissing him, being kissed, and the dazzling light all around them.

And then, out of nowhere, there was a huge bump, like a ship knocking into them, and they both lurched to one side.

'What the—?'

Magnus, bored, was looking for attention, and was rubbing his great rump against Lex, who drew a long and not entirely steady breath and let Romy go.

'I think maybe I needed that, Magnus,' he said.

Romy swallowed. She felt jarred, as if she had been on a spinning roundabout that had suddenly stopped, and it was all she could do not to throw herself back into Lex's arms.

But that would be a very, very bad idea, she remembered. Because they weren't in Paris now. They were in Scotland, and it was twelve years later and very cold, and they were just pretending. It had just been a kiss for show, in case Willie was watching.

Hadn't it?

She moistened her lips. 'We'd better go in,' she said, barely registering the dog gambolling beside them. 'Freya might be awake.'

'Yes,' said Lex, 'perhaps we better had.'

What chance had he had of working after that? Lex switched off the light and climbed into bed beside Romy. It had been madness to kiss her out there in the snow, but he hadn't been able to stop himself. She had been so close, so perfect, and it had felt so right. The feel of her, the taste of her had set tremors going in his heart. He could almost hear it cracking.

It had been his own fault. He should have stayed inside and worked, the way he had intended to do. But when they came back to the house, and Romy went off to find Freya, instead of sitting down at his computer and emailing Summer, Lex had wandered around, eventually finding himself in a room that was empty of all but a few chairs and a piano.

And not just any piano. A Bösendorfer, no less.

Lex had a grand in his penthouse apartment, but it wasn't as big as this one. To Lex, it seemed to exert a pull that drew him across the room, to run his hand over its gleaming mahogany top and then lift the lid to press a key, then another and another. Without quite knowing how it had happened, Lex found himself sitting on the stool and letting his fingers run over the keys and then he was playing.

He played out the tumult of feeling inside him that had gripped him ever since Romy had ducked her head and stepped into the cabin. He played out the memory of her touch, the way she made him feel, and then, so gradually he hardly noticed that he was doing it, he started to play the strange feeling of liberation that morning, that sense of being dropped into a different world, isolated by the snow, where all the usual rules were suspended.

And after a while, the tune changed again, to echo old Scottish folk songs that he had once learnt, and to play out the glittering morning and the air and the hills and the water, and Romy, laughing in the snow.

Lex played on, absorbed in the music, unaware of anyone else until a movement from doorway made him look up. Willie was there, listening, and the grief in his eyes made Lex's fingers still.

'I'm sorry,' he said. 'I should have asked if I could use the piano.'

Willie waved the apology aside. 'I'm glad you did. I haven't heard it since Moira died, but I can't bring myself to get rid it.'

He asked if Lex would play again that evening, and Lex was glad to. He didn't normally like performing for an audience, but playing was better than sitting next to Romy and feeling his hands itch with the need to touch her. Better than having to pretend to her that he didn't want her, while pretending to Willie that he did.

He found some music in the piano stool, and played the most battered scores, which he guessed would have been Moira Grant's favourites. Romy sat next to Willie and held his hand while the tears rolled down his face.

'Thank you,' he said simply when Lex had finished. 'I'm glad you came. I'm glad my store's going to be run by a man who can play like that.'

The thaw had set in already. By lunchtime, the glittering morning had vanished beneath the cloud cover, and the temperature had risen with remarkable speed. Tomorrow, it was clear, they would be able to leave. Lex lay in the dark and listened to the steady drip, drip, drip of melting snow outside the window.

Get through tonight, he told himself. That's all you have to do.

Beside him, Romy was concentrating on

breathing very quietly. The curtains hanging round the bed smelt musty, but the sheets were clean and faintly scented. The mattress was comfortable. It was dark. She had hardly slept the night before and now she was very tired.

There was no reason why she shouldn't be able to sleep.

Except the memory of that kiss that had been thrumming beneath her skin all day. And then Lex's playing had stirred up emotions Romy had rather left buried. She hadn't been able to take her eyes off his hands while he was playing, hadn't been able to stop remembering those long, dextrous fingers smoothing and stroking, exploring her, unlocking her.

Stop thinking about it, she told herself. Get through tonight. That's all you have to do.

CHAPTER SEVEN

AFRAID to move in case she disturbed Lex, Romy stared into the darkness and told herself to be sensible while the silence lengthened, stretched, and at last grew so painful that she couldn't bear it any more.

'Lex?' she asked quietly, just in case he was asleep after all.

There was a tiny pause, and then he let out a breath. 'Yes?'

'You're not asleep?'

'No.'

'Neither am I.'

'I gathered that.' Lex sounded resigned. Or amused. Or exasperated. Or maybe all three.

Romy sighed and rolled onto her side to face him through the darkness. 'I can't sleep. I keep thinking about that kiss this morning.'

'That was a mistake,' he said after a moment.

'Was it?'

She could just make out his profile. He wasn't looking at her. He was looking up at the ceiling. 'I've spent twelve years trying to forget Paris,' he said. 'Trying to forget *you*. One kiss, and I might as well not have bothered.'

He sounded bitter, and Romy bit her lip.

'I think about that time too,' she said quietly. 'I think the reason I can't forget it is because we never ended it properly. You just…left. We never talked about it, never had a chance to say goodbye.'

'What was the point of talking?' asked Lex. 'You didn't want to be with me. You wanted to make a life on your own, and you were right. There was no point in me staying. It was over.'

'It didn't feel over,' said Romy. 'It didn't feel over this morning when we kissed.'

There was a silence, loud with memories. Then Lex turned and lay on his side so that they faced each other at last. 'Do you remember what you said out there in the snow? You said that I wasn't afraid of anything.'

'I remember,' she said softly.

'I'm afraid of how I felt about you. I'm afraid of feeling that way again.' The words came out stiffly, forced through tight lips as if against his will. 'I don't want to fall in love with you again, Romy,' he said.

Romy drew a breath, heart cracking at the suppressed pain in his voice. 'I don't want to fall in love with you either,' she told him. 'I don't want to need you. I don't want to need anybody.' She swallowed. 'I'm not suggesting we try again. It didn't work twelve years ago, and it's not going to work now. We both know that.'

She could feel Lex's eyes on her face through the darkness, sense the tautness of his body. 'What *are* you suggesting?' he asked.

'That we have one more night,' said Romy. 'One last time together and, this time, we'll end it properly. Tomorrow, we'll say goodbye and draw a line under everything we've had together. We can get on with our lives without wondering how it would have been.'

Hardly able to believe how calm she sounded when her pulse was booming and thumping, she edged towards the middle of the bed. 'We could think of it as closure.'

Lex shifted over the mattress and laid his palm against her cheek in the darkness, feeling her quiver at his touch. 'Closure,' he repeated, as if trying out the word.

He liked the idea. One last night. No more wondering, no more regretting. Just accepting at long last that it was over.

'It's just been such a strange day,' said Romy, lifting her hand to his wrist, unable to stop herself touching him in return. 'I've felt unreal all day, as if I've stepped into a different world.'

'I know what you mean.' They were very close now. Lex let his fingers slide under her hair, curl around the soft nape of her neck, and her hand was drifting up to his shoulder. 'As if the normal rules don't apply today.'

'Exactly,' she said unevenly.

'Tomorrow, we're going back to the real world.' Already he was unwinding her sarong, his hand warm and sure, curving now around her breast, dipping into her waist, over her hip and then slipping possessively to the base of her spine to pull her closer. 'Tomorrow, we go back to normal.'

'I know.'

Romy's senses were reeling. She had a vague sense that they should be talking this through properly, but how could she talk when he was smoothing possessively down her thigh to the back of her knee and up again, gentling up her spine, making her gasp with the warmth of his hand? When he was rolling her onto her back, when she was pulling him over her? When he was pressing his mouth to the curve of her neck so that she sucked in a breath and arched beneath him.

'It's just tonight,' she managed, barely aware of what she was saying, loving his warm, sleek weight on her, loving the feel of his back beneath her hands, the flex of response when she trailed her fingers up his flank. It felt so right to touch him again that her heart squeezed and she could hardly breathe with it.

'Just tonight,' Lex murmured agreement against her throat.

Beneath his hands, beneath the wicked pleasure of his lips, Romy felt all thought evaporate. There was only Lex and the heat and the rush and the wild joy, so she didn't even hear when he said it again. 'Tomorrow, it'll be over.'

The car was packed. Freya, strapped firmly in, was kicking her heels petulantly against the car seat, her face screwed up in sullen protest. When Willie waved through the window, she refused to smile back at him.

The crispness of the day before had vanished under thick grey cloud. There was still snow, but it was slumped and saggy now. Great clumps kept slipping off the branches in a shower of white.

Romy kissed Willie affectionately as she said goodbye, and even managed a brief pat for Magnus.

Lex shook Willie's hand. 'Thank you,' he said. 'Thank you for everything. It's been a pleasure doing business with you.'

'Likewise,' said Willie, wringing his hand in

return. 'I'm glad to know my stores will be in good hands.'

'We'll let the lawyers draw up the contract, then, when we're both happy with it, we'll arrange a formal signing.' Lex was all business this morning. 'I presume that you would like that to take place here?'

'Well, I've been thinking about that,' said Willie, 'and I've decided that I should come to London.'

'To London?' Lex repeated, not quite succeeding in keeping the consternation from his voice. 'I wouldn't ask you to do that, Willie. I'm very happy to come back here, honestly.'

'No, I'd like to,' Willie said. He looked from Romy to Lex, who were carefully not looking at each other. 'Seeing you two together, hearing you play piano... I'm not sure how to explain, but you've made me realise that it's time to start living again,' he told them.

'Ever since Moira died, I've been hiding away here, but she wouldn't have wanted that. She used to like to go to London. We always stayed at Claridges.' He nodded firmly, mind made up. 'I'll stay there. I'll sign the contract. I'll see you both again, and Freya, I hope. It'll be good for me.'

There was a pause. Afraid that Willie would hear the dismay in it, Romy rushed to fill the silence. 'Well...that's great, Willie. You must come to dinner. I don't think Claridges is quite ready for Freya yet.'

Willie beamed. 'That would be very nice.'

Lex was left with little choice. 'We'll look forward to it,' he said.

There was silence in the car as they bumped carefully down the track. Willie was lost to sight and they were turning onto the single track road before Romy spoke.

'Now what?' she asked.

'Now we go back to London.'

'You know what I mean. Willie's coming to London. He's going to expect to see us together.'

'He is,' Lex agreed grimly. 'Especially now you've invited him to dinner.'

'I had to! It would have looked really odd if neither of us said anything, when we've been staying with him and drinking all his whisky.'

'I suppose so.' Lex's mouth was pulled down at the corners, his brows drawn together in an irritable line. 'But now we're going to have to stay a couple until this bloody contract is signed, and who knows how long it will be before we can do that. Once the lawyers get their hands on it, it could be months!'

'Months?' Romy was dismayed.

'Weeks, anyway.'

'Whatever happened to "tomorrow it'll be over"?' She sighed.

It was the first time either of them had referred to the night before. When Romy stirred that morning, Lex had already showered and shaved. His face was set, his eyes shuttered, and she could see that it was over, just as they had agreed.

Romy told herself that she was glad that he was sticking to their agreement. Closure, wasn't that what she had called it? Easy to say before his mouth was hot and wicked against her, before the heat and the wildness drove them into a different place where there was nothing but touching and feeling and the heart-stopping joy of *now*.

If Lex had woken her with a kiss, if he had touched her at all and suggested that they made love one more time… Romy wanted to think that she would have been strong enough and sensible enough to resist, but she wasn't sure.

'It *is* over,' said Lex, without taking his eyes from the road. 'Last night was about us. This is about business. We've started on a pretence and now we're going to have to keep it going. It would have been fine if Willie had stayed at Duncardie like he was supposed to, but too many people in London will be able to tell him we're nothing to do with each other.'

'We told him we were keeping it a secret,' Romy pointed out.

'No relationship is that secret. Even Willie is

going to wonder why no one at all has any inkling that we've even met, let alone are engaged. I'm not prepared to take that risk,' said Lex. 'If Willie even suspects that we've been pretending, it would be even worse than if we'd told him the truth about my lack of family man credentials in the first place.'

'Oh, dear,' Romy sighed again. 'I wish now I'd been straight with him right at the start.'

'It's too late for wishing,' Lex said. 'We're stuck with this pretence now, and we'll have to see it through to the bitter end. It's not as if I'm a monster. I may not be prepared to share my life with a kid, but that doesn't mean I send little boys up chimneys. Gibson & Grieve have plenty of family-friendly policies, as you pointed out. It's a good deal for Grant's Supersavers as well as for us.'

Part of Romy marvelled that they were able to talk so dispassionately about the situation. It was bizarre to be having such a practical conversation when last night… But there was no point in thinking about last night, she caught herself up quickly. Much better to be talking about how they were going to handle the pretence than to sit here in silence, her body still thrumming, remembering, and reminding herself of all the reasons why it was sensible that they never made love again.

I don't want to fall in love with you again, Lex

had said. Until then, Romy hadn't appreciated just how much she had hurt him. She couldn't do that to him again.

And she couldn't hurt herself. The need to protect herself was too deeply engrained for Romy to be able to contemplate loving Lex the way he deserved to be loved. To risk *needing* him. She would be too exposed when it ended, as end it would.

How could it last when they were so different, when they wanted such different things? Lex couldn't have made it clearer. He wasn't prepared to share his life with a child.

Romy glanced over her shoulder at Freya, who had fallen asleep before they got to the road. The sight of her daughter steadied her. Even if Lex changed his mind, even if she were brave enough to take the risk for herself, she still wouldn't do it. If Freya spent too much time with Lex, she would learn to love him. That was what children did. And then, when he left, when he couldn't bear the mess and the noise any longer, her heart would break. Romy knew what it felt like to be abandoned. She wouldn't let that happen to her daughter.

She turned back to face the front, and glanced at Lex. 'OK, we're stuck with it,' she said briskly. *This is about business*, he had said. Business it would be. 'What do you suggest?'

'I think you—and Freya—should move into my flat.'

'I'm not sure that's a good idea,' said Romy.

'Why not?'

'People at work will realise. Someone's bound to see us.'

'That's the whole point,' he said irritably. 'We want them to realise. Then when Willie turns up, nobody is going to act surprised if we're together. And you and Freya are there when he comes to this dinner you've invited him to.'

Romy stuck out her bottom lip. 'But that's weeks away! Why can't I stay in my flat, and just come and cook dinner that night?'

'Because nobody is going to believe that we're a real couple if you're flogging back to your flat. When are we supposed to have this mad, passionate affair if you're spending two hours every day on the Northern Line?'

'Nobody needs to know where I'm going,' she said stubbornly, and Lex threw her a disbelieving glance.

'Want a bet?'

Romy folded her arms crossly. She could see it made sense, but living with Lex for weeks on end, trying not to think about touching him, trying not to remember… How was she going to bear it?

'Are you sure you've thought this through?' she

said. 'You think there's a lot of Freya's stuff in the back, but that's what we needed for a night away. Imagine what we'll need if we're staying for weeks.'

'I'm not expecting to enjoy the experience,' said Lex, 'but if it means the deal with Grant's Supersavers goes through, then I'll put up with it.'

'And what about me?'

'What do you mean?'

'What do I get out of it?'

'You get a fantastic reference, and the experience of working on a successful project,' said Lex. 'That's worth a lot when you're looking for a good job.'

Romy knew that it was true. She badly needed both. She had had a lovely time drifting around the world, but she was ill equipped when it came to supporting her daughter. Phin's offer of a temporary job with Gibson & Grieve had been a godsend, but finding a well-paid permanent job would be more of a challenge.

And even if she hadn't needed something impressive on her CV, there was Tim and the rest of the acquisitions team to think about. They had made her welcome, taught her all they knew. They needed the deal with Grant's Supersavers to go through, too. She couldn't let them down either.

'All right,' she said, turning her bracelets as she tried to think it through. 'Freya and I move in with you. We let people think we're living together. Fine. How long before our mothers get wind of it?'

'Oh, God,' said Lex. He hadn't thought about his mother. Or Romy's mother. The mothers together. 'Oh, God,' he said again.

'We can't tell them the truth.'

He actually blanched. 'God, no!'

'So that means they're going to have to believe that we're in love,' Romy went on remorselessly.

'Oh, no…' He could see exactly where she was going with this.

'And *that* will mean that there'll be hell to pay when it turns out that we're not getting married after all.'

Lex gripped the steering wheel, his knuckles white as he imagined the scene in appalling detail. 'We'll just have to say that it didn't work out,' he said. 'We'll say it was a mutual decision.'

'I could say that I wanted to take Freya to be near her father,' Romy offered. 'I've been thinking that's what I should do anyway.'

There was a tiny pause. 'That would work,' Lex agreed tonelessly.

'But your mother will be furious with me.'

'I'll tell her I don't care,' he said. 'I'll say that I couldn't cope with living with a baby. She'll believe that.'

It was Romy's turn to pause. 'There you are then.'

Lex shot her a swift penetrating look, then fixed his eyes on the road once more. Neither of them said anything about the night before.

'Problem solved,' he said.

'Where would you like to sleep?'

It had been a long day. The drive to Inverness, the flight back to London, and then, deciding to get all the upheaval over with in one fell swoop, the limousine that picked them up from the airport had detoured via Romy's flat so that she could pack up everything she would need for the next few weeks.

Now they stood in Lex's penthouse flat, surrounded by a sea of bags and toys and bumper packs of nappies. Freya's things looked even more incongruous here than they had done at Duncardie. Holding Freya in her arms, Romy looked around her, impressed and chilled in equal measure.

The living area was a huge open space with a whole wall of glass looking out over the Thames. There was a grand piano in one corner, a sleek leather sofa, a black-granite-topped table with striking chairs. No clutter, no mess, no softness or colour. Hard edges wherever she looked. It was hard to imagine anywhere less suitable for a crawling baby.

'What's the choice?' she asked.

'There are two spare rooms,' said Lex. 'So you

can sleep with Freya, sleep on your own.' He hesitated. 'Or sleep with me.'

Romy stilled. 'I thought it was over.'

'It was. It is.' He moved restlessly. 'It should be.'

All the way home he had been wrestling with memories of the night before. Closure? Hah! How could there be closure when Romy was sitting beside him, when the feel of her, the taste of her, was imprinted on his body and on his mind?

'I just thought…if we're going to be living together…' He dragged his fingers through his hair, not really knowing what he was trying to say. At least, he knew what, but not how to say it. 'It was good, wasn't it?'

'Yes.' Romy set Freya on the floor, where she immediately set about unpacking toys from one of the bags, throwing them all over Lex's pristine carpet. 'It was too good,' she said.

Hugging her arms together, she stepped over the bags and wandered over to the huge window. 'It would be so easy to spend the next few weeks together, Lex. It would be good again—it would be wonderful, probably—but how would we stop then?'

'Maybe we wouldn't want to.'

'Look at all this stuff!' Romy swung round and gestured at the sea of bags and baby gear. 'We've only been here five minutes and already your flat looks like a bomb has hit it. How are you going to cope with this level of mess for weeks on end?'

Her eyes rested on her daughter, who had discovered a much-loved floppy rabbit and was sucking its already battered ear. 'Freya isn't always as happy as this,' she told Lex. 'Sometimes she wakes in the nights, and the screaming will sound like a drill in your head. There'll be dirty nappies and sticky fingers all over your furniture... You'll hate it!'

She tried to smile. 'Remember how you said you would tell your mother that you couldn't cope with living with a baby? I don't think you'll have any difficulty sounding convincing about that.'

'Perhaps you're right.' Lex rubbed a hand over his face in a gesture of weary resignation. 'I know you're right, in fact.'

'We may be different, but we're the same in one way,' said Romy. 'We're both afraid of getting too involved. Me because I'm afraid of being hurt, and you because you're afraid of the mess that comes along with any kind of relationship. You could say that we're made for each other,' she added with a crooked smile.

'Neither of us is prepared to commit to a relationship that we're not sure will last, but, apart from that, what have we got in common?' Romy went on, still hugging her arms together as she paced restlessly around the immaculate room.

'This apartment is so you, Lex. It's cool and it's calm and it's perfectly ordered. I can see why you like it like this, but it's no place for Freya, and if it's no place for her, it's no place for me. So we'll be leaving as soon as Willie has signed that contract. And the more nights we have like last one, the harder it will be to say goodbye.'

She was terribly afraid of falling in love with him. She was afraid of needing him. Surely Lex could see that?

'You're right,' said Lex again. He straightened his shoulders. 'It would be a big mistake. Madness. What was I thinking?'

He looked across the room into Romy's dark eyes and knew exactly what he had been thinking. He had been thinking about the satiny warmth of her skin. About the heat and the piercing sweetness and the aching sense of peace when he lay with his face buried in her throat.

He hadn't been thinking about reality. He hadn't been thinking about business.

Fool.

'I'm sorry,' he said to Romy. 'Really sorry. Forget I suggested it. Let's make it easy on ourselves, and stick to business from now on.'

Over the years, Romy had slept in bus stations and on beaches. She had spent nights cold and muddy and soaking wet, huddled under rocks on a hillside, or swiping at mosquitoes in the rainforest. Every single one of those long, uncomfortable nights had been easier than the ones she spent in Lex's apartment, trying to sleep in the room next to his and thinking about how close he was.

Thinking about how easy it would be to slip into bed beside him, and whisper that she had changed her mind, that nothing could be harder than never touching him again.

But Romy only had to think about Freya to remember that of course there could be something harder. There could be seeing her daughter hurt and lost, looking for someone who wasn't there, just as she had once looked for her father after he had left.

It was the strangest month of Romy's life. During the day, she went to the office, just as she had done before, and collected Freya from the crèche at half past five. But instead of squeezing onto the tube with all the other commuters to get back to the poky rented flat that was all she had been able to afford, she put Freya in the pushchair and walked back to Lex's luxury apartment.

They decided not to make an announcement about their supposed relationship, but wait for speculation and gossip to start circulating around the office. Romy assumed this would happen very quickly, but it took a surprisingly long time for her colleagues to suspect that anything might have occurred between her and Lex on the trip to Scotland.

This might have had something to do with the fact that Lex ignored her completely at the office. Romy returned to a heroine's welcome the day after their return. Her fellow members of the acquisitions team were full of admiration.

'How brave of you to spend all that time with Lex Gibson,' was the typical reaction. 'I'd have been terrified!' And then, leaning closer, 'What was he like?'

Romy thought about Lex in the snow, grinning as he held the snowball over her. She thought about him struggling to change Freya's nappy, his hair on end and his tie askew. She thought about the way his hand had skimmed lovingly over her hip, his slow smile as he drew her to him again, and her throat closed.

'He was fine.'

'I hear he's coming to the meeting this morning. He must be pleased with us. He *never* leaves his office!'

There was much shuffling and straightening of ties when Lex appeared at the departmental meeting. He had a formidable presence, Romy thought, trying to see him through her colleagues' eyes. He wasn't particularly tall or particularly handsome, but he had an air of cool authority that meant he dominated a room just by walking into it.

To the others, their chief executive must look austere and remote. His manner was brusque, and with that severe expression, the inflexible mouth, and those unnervingly pale eyes, it was easy to see how he had gained a reputation as an unfeeling tyrant. Lex might be respected, even admired, by his staff, but he wasn't liked. He lacked his brother Phin's easy charm.

But when Romy's eyes rested on his stern mouth, her heart crumbled. When she watched his hands, a flood of warmth dissolved her bones. She shifted uneasily in her chair, convinced that everyone must be able to see her glowing, *humming* with awareness of him, but no one was looking at her. Their attention was focused on Lex, who outlined the discussions at Duncardie and congratulated Tim and the team on their hard work setting up the deal.

'Perhaps we should make a special mention of Romy?' said Tim, who had thanked Romy effusively earlier. 'I'm certainly very grateful to her for stepping in at the last moment.'

Then, of course, they *did* all look at her. There were some smiles and even winks from those in no danger of being seen by Lex.

'Indeed.' Lex's eyes rested indifferently on Romy's burning face. 'She was very helpful.'

Helpful! Romy's lips tightened with annoyance. Couldn't he have found something a little less chilly to say? What was wrong with, I couldn't have done it without her, for instance? Nobody was ever going to guess they were having an affair if he carried on like that!

It was clear that the others thought he could have been more effusive, too. There was a slightly awkward pause.

'Well…well done, everybody!' Tim brought the meeting to a close. 'I think a team outing is called for.' He raised a hand to quell the stir of anticipation before it got out of hand. 'Keep next Friday free and we'll celebrate in style.'

Lex got to his feet. 'Good work,' he said to everyone and that cool gaze didn't even pause on Romy as it swept impersonally round the room. 'Enjoy yourselves next Friday. You've deserved it.'

Correctly interpreting this to mean that, (a) he wasn't planning on spoiling their fun by turning up, and, (b) the celebratory bash would be covered by the company, everyone relaxed and a buzz of conversation and laughter broke out the moment Lex had left the room.

Romy forced herself to join in, but it was an effort. Reluctant as she was to admit it, she was miffed. Lex shouldn't have been able to look at her with that expression of utter indifference, not when she had been sitting there positively throbbing with awareness!

She was still feeling cross that evening when Lex came home. She had just finished bathing Freya and the sound of the door opening made her heart jerk, which did nothing to improve her temper.

Well, she wasn't going to rush out and welcome him home, Romy decided. If he thought she was going to have his pipe and slippers ready for him, he had another think coming! Trying to ignore the knotting of her entrails, she finished tidying the bathroom before she picked up Freya and made her way out to the open plan living area.

Lex was in the kitchen at the black granite worktop that divided the cooking from the living area. Romy had cooked Freya macaroni cheese for her supper earlier, and the counter behind him was still cluttered with open packets of butter and flour, with milk and cheese and apple cores. Wisely, Lex had turned his back on the mess and was reading his post, but he looked up when Romy appeared.

'Oh. Hello,' she said, deliberately cool.

Unfortunately, Freya was sending out a very different message by beaming at him in a way that disconcerted Lex quite as much as it annoyed Romy.

Freya had only just learnt to flirt, and had spent most of the flight home the day before practising on him. There had been a lot of smiling and peeping glances under her lashes. Quite why her daughter had picked Lex as a favourite, Romy wasn't sure. He certainly did nothing to encourage her. It was clear, in fact, that all the attention made him uneasy, but Freya was undeterred by his lack of response.

Now here she was, looking delighted to see that he was home, while he just stood there looking dour! Quickly, Romy put her on the floor with all her toys, where she was soon diverted.

CHAPTER EIGHT

'HELLO,' said Lex, dropping the credit-card statement he'd been studying onto the worktop. There was no mistaking the coolness in Romy's voice, and he eyed her warily. 'How did you get on today?'

'Well, I spent most of it accepting commiserations about having to spend three whole days with you,' said Romy. She moved past him to start clearing up the debris from Freya's supper. 'Having seen the way you barely recognised me in that meeting, they all think you ignored me the whole time. If you want word to get round that we're a couple, you're going to have to try harder than that!'

Lex wrenched at his tie to loosen it. 'I thought we'd decided not to make an announcement?'

'Yes, because we want people to guess and start gossiping. They're never going to guess if you look through me and have trouble remembering my name! You had the perfect opportunity to hint that you think I'm special, but no! *"She was very helpful,"'* Romy mimicked his austere tones as she scraped the last few pieces of pasta from Freya's bowl and let the bin close with a rattle. 'Was that really the best you could do?'

'What did you want me to do? Throw you across the table and ravish you in front of all your colleagues?'

'A smile would have done it.' Romy began closing packets and putting everything away. 'That would have been so unusual they'd all have twigged straight away that there was something going on. As it was, none of them have a clue!'

'Well, I'm sorry,' said Lex stiffly, 'but it felt awkward.'

'You can say that again. I'm now the person who can spend three days with her boss without him realising that I even exist!'

Lex rolled his shoulders uncomfortably. 'I suppose I was thrown,' he admitted. 'I knew you'd be there, of course, but it was…odd…seeing you in a work context.'

A little mollified, Romy wrung out a cloth and wiped down the counter. 'I'd say you'd have to try harder next time, but we're not likely to have another meeting together, are we? We managed to work in the same office for six months without even seeing each other. I wonder if we should go in together for a few days? Someone is bound to notice that.'

Lex was usually at the office by seven o'clock, but the next morning found him walking into the gleaming reception area with Romy almost two hours later. Normally, he would stride straight to the lifts, with a brief nod of acknowledgement to whoever was on Reception. There weren't many other people around at that time and that was the way Lex liked it.

Now he felt extraordinarily self-conscious. Although no one actually stopped and pointed, he could tell that his arrival with Romy—and a push-chair!—had indeed been noted and would provide food for much comment and speculation by the coffee machines that morning.

'Well,' said Romy awkwardly. 'I'd…er…I'd better take Freya to the crèche.' Burningly aware of the covert stares in her direction—why on earth had she suggested this?—she mustered a smile. 'See you later.'

'Do you think I should kiss you?' Lex muttered and her heart promptly performed a back flip that threw out her breathing completely.

'*Kiss* me?'

'We're making an exhibition of ourselves just by standing here,' he said, still talking out of the corner of his mouth. 'We might as well really give them all something to talk about. You were the one keen to get the message across that I know you exist. I mean, that's what couples do, isn't it?' he added when she hesitated. 'Kiss each other goodbye?'

Romy swallowed. 'Usually just a peck on the lips.'

'I wasn't thinking of sweeping you into my arms!'

Her colour deepened at the sardonic note in his voice. 'Of course not.' She cleared her throat. 'OK, then.'

Lex put a hand at the small of her back to draw her closer and she lifted her face. It was ridiculous. They had kissed before. This would just be a brief brush of the lips.

But still her pulse was booming so loudly that the hubbub in Reception faded to nothing in comparison, and when he pressed his mouth to hers her hand rose instinctively to clutch at the sleeve of his jacket. The polished marble floor still seemed to drop away beneath her feet, and she was still intensely aware of the firmness and warmth of his lips, of the steely strength of his arm.

And when Lex lifted his head, she still felt hot and dizzy.

Lex's expression was impenetrable as he let her go. 'See you tonight,' he said coolly and walked off to the lifts, leaving Romy to make her way to the crèche with burning cheeks.

* * *

'Did that kiss this morning do the trick?' Lex asked that night as he pulled off his tie.

Romy had hoped to have the kitchen tidy before he got home, but she was still washing up. At least it gave her a good excuse to stand with her back to him so that, after a quick greeting over her shoulder, he couldn't read her expression.

Ever since she had brought Freya home earlier, she had been practising how she would be when Lex appeared. Her lips had been tingling from that one brief kiss all day, and she was annoyed with herself for letting it affect her so much. Not that she had any intention of letting Lex guess that. She could do cool, too.

'It certainly did,' she said, proud of her casual tone. 'It must have taken all of two seconds for the news that you had kissed me in Reception to reach Acquisitions. Then, of course, I had to spend all day fending off questions and explaining why I hadn't told them about you.'

'What did you say?'

'The truth.'

'*What?*'

'Oh, not about the pretence.' Romy rinsed Freya's plate under the tap. 'Just that we'd known each other a long time ago, and got together again on the trip to Scotland.' She glanced at him over her shoulder again. 'I don't suppose anyone dared ask *you* about it?'

'No, but Summer smiled at me in a very knowing way.' Lex was regarding the chaos in the living area with dismay. 'Thank God Phin is out of contact in Africa. Summer's extraordinarily discreet, but she's bound to tell him, and then it'll only be a matter of time before my mother knows, and then *your* mother will know, and then there'll be no end to it.' He sighed and dragged a hand through his hair.

'We'll tell them we wanted to keep it a secret,' said Romy.

'So secret that I kissed you in the middle of Reception in front of half the staff?'

'Well, it's done now.' Romy dried her hands on a tea towel and turned. 'We went through all of this,' she reminded him.

'I know.'

Restless, Lex hunched his shoulders. He had been like this all day, ever since that damned kiss. No one had *said* anything, but he could tell that speculation was rife and that behind the bland expressions they were all wondering what on earth had happened to turn their tough chief executive into the kind of sap who kissed his girlfriend in front of his entire staff.

Lex cringed inwardly at the memory. What had

he been thinking? He had humiliated himself in public, and for what? The chance to kiss Romy one more time.

Pathetic.

Surely he had had enough rejection. He had suggested they make the most of the time they had together, and Romy had said no. How many times did she have to tell him that they had no future together? How many times did he have to tell *himself*?

And still he only had to touch her, and reason evaporated. Romy would never know what an effort it had been to keep that kiss brief. It had been all Lex could do not to pull her down onto the floor, and to hell with their audience.

That would have given them all something to talk about!

Lex sighed. Continuing the pretence had seemed to make sense, but if they weren't careful it would spiral out of control. The very thought of losing control made him shudder, but what could he do? They couldn't stop now.

And it would be worth it when Willie Grant finally signed that contract, Lex reminded himself as he picked his way across the floor.

Freya, newly bathed and with a quiff of dark hair sticking up, was sitting in the middle of a sea of toys. She offered him a toothless smile but didn't clamour to be held the way she had the day before.

Well, good.

Just as well, thought Lex. He had no intention of picking her up.

So why did it feel like yet another rejection?

Splashing water on his face in his bathroom, Lex pulled himself together. The deal, that was all that mattered. Once it was done, Romy and Freya would leave, and his life could go back to normal. Until then, he would just have to put up with the humiliation and the mess and this feeling that everything was on the point of slipping out of control.

Romy was still clearing the kitchen when he went out. For the first time in his life, Lex had found it hard to concentrate at the office, and he had brought a report home to read, but the chances of concentration here were even slimmer until Freya had gone to bed, he realised.

His space invaded on every front, Lex took refuge at the piano. Alone in the evenings he would sit and play to unwind from work. Perhaps it would help now.

He played a few chords softly, letting his fingers warm up and go where they would, but he had barely started before there was a tugging at his trouser leg as Freya desperately hauled herself upright, loudly demanding to be lifted up to the source of the magical sounds.

'Freya!' Realising too late what was happening, Romy hurried over to take her away. 'Leave Lex alone! I'm sorry,' she added to Lex as Freya wailed in protest.

'Oh, let her come up if she's so insistent,' he said brusquely. 'Here—' He held out his arms, and after a moment's hesitation Romy put Freya in them.

Freya's tears cleared magically as Lex settled her on his lap and let her lean forward to crash her little hands onto the piano keys.

Wincing at the noise, Romy perched on the arm of a sofa and watched as Lex let Freya bash away for a minute or so before he took her hands very gently and helped her to press the keys properly. Freya's expression was transfigured as she heard the notes sing out from beneath her fingers, and Romy felt her throat tighten at his patience with her daughter.

Naturally, Freya's attention span was limited, and she was soon back to 'playing' on her own. 'I hope she's not damaging your piano,' Romy said, raising her voice over the crashing chords.

'She's all right,' said Lex. 'It's a good thing to let her get used to just sitting at a piano if she likes it. Maybe she's going to be musical.'

Romy opened her mouth to suggest that he could

teach Freya to play properly when she was a bit older, but shut it again almost immediately. What was she thinking? By the time Freya was old enough to learn the piano, they would be long gone.

'She wouldn't get it from me,' she said instead.

'Perhaps her father is musical,' Lex said evenly.

'Perhaps. I must ask him.' Romy shifted on the arm of the sofa. 'If I remember, I'll ask him this weekend.'

Lex looked up sharply. 'This weekend?'

'Yes, I…I emailed Michael this morning.'

She shouldn't feel awkward about it, Romy knew. It was past time for her to let Michael know that he was a father. She had been putting it off because it felt as if she would somehow lose some of her independence if he decided he wanted to be part of Freya's life.

Whichever way she looked at it, a relationship between Freya and her father would be a tie. Never again would Romy be able to move on the moment it suited her. There would always be someone else to take into account. Of course, she had to take Freya into account now, but it wasn't the same.

What if Michael wanted to see Freya regularly? What if he wanted a say in where she lived or where she went to school? Romy knew that she ought to be glad if it turned out that he wanted to be involved in his daughter's life, but she hated the idea of anyone limiting her freedom in any way. She knew it wasn't logical or justifiable or fair, but the prospect of involving anyone else in the life she had built with Freya smacked too much of commitment for Romy.

And yet, today she had emailed him. It didn't make Romy feel any better to realise that she had only done it because she had been so thrown by that kiss this morning.

It was stupid. It hadn't meant anything, but she hadn't been able to get it out of her mind all day. This was just what Romy had been afraid of. She didn't want her pulse to jump every time Lex walked into a room. She didn't want to be waiting for him, looking for him, unable to settle unless he was there. Next thing she knew, she would be hopelessly in love with him. She would be needing a man who had been very straight about not wanting anything to do with a baby.

Romy knew how that would end. So she had done what she always did when she felt herself getting too close to anyone. She made her plans to move on.

'I asked if we could meet,' she told Lex. 'He replied straight away.'

Lex's head was bent over Freya's as he guided her hands on the piano keys. 'Did you tell him about Freya?'

'Not yet. I thought it would be better to tell him face to face. I've got a friend who lives in Taunton, which isn't far from Michael. I'm going to stay with her tomorrow, and she's going to look after Freya while I go and see him on Sunday morning. It might be too much of a shock if I turned up with her.' Romy had a nasty feeling that she was babbling, and made herself stop.

'He must be keen if he's meeting you at such short notice,' said Lex after a moment. 'You've arranged it all very quickly.'

'Well, I've waited long enough. I thought I might get too nervous if I had to think about what to say to him for too long.' Romy fiddled with her bracelets. 'Besides, I thought it might be nice for you to have the flat to yourself for the weekend.'

'Thanks for the thought, but I won't be here myself. I was going to say the same to you.'

'Oh?' Her fingers stilled. 'Where are you going?'

'To visit my parents, who I sincerely hope won't have heard any rumours about our supposed relationship just yet.' Lex's smile gleamed briefly, but without much humour. 'I'll be able to tell my father about the deal with Willie Grant. It looks as if both of us will be passing on surprising news this weekend, doesn't it?'

* * *

Lex drove back to London early on Sunday afternoon. A chance for some time to himself, he had decided. Some quiet. Some order. To catch up on some work. To walk across his living room without tripping over a squeaky toy and to admire his spectacular view without Freya squealing and shouting in the background.

But when he let himself into the flat, it didn't feel quiet. It felt empty.

Romy and Freya had only been in residence two days. What was it going to be like when they left after a month?

By then he would be desperate for some peace, Lex told himself. He would be sick of tripping over the pushchair every time he came through the door. He could take those rounded rubber clips off the corners of the coffee table, and the plastic covers off his state-of-the art steel sockets. The waxed tablecloth with its pattern of brightly coloured dots would be gone, and he would be able to see his stylish dining table again.

There would be no little clothes drying on airers. No baby food in the fridge. No toys scattered on the floor or plastic ducks in the bath.

No Freya.

No Romy.

Lex could smell her perfume in the air. She was such a vivid presence that her absence was a shout in the silence. He could picture her exactly, barefoot, swinging Freya into the air, dark eyes aglow.

Was he going to have to endure another twelve years of memories? Twelve years of remembering the nape of her neck, the back of her knee, the scent of her hair. And this time it would be worse, Lex knew. Now he knew there was more to Romy than that wild, passionate girl she had been at eighteen. She was intelligent and capable and charming. She was warm. She was practical. She was tender.

And she was so damned stubborn.

Romy would never change her mind. If she said she would leave, she would leave. He had better get used to it.

Alarmed at the maudlin train of his thoughts, Lex pulled himself together sharply. Why was he feeling so glum? He had what he wanted. What he *needed*. He had the Grant's Supersaver deal in his pocket. He had control of Gibson & Grieve. Control of his life. No one asking anything of him that he couldn't give.

What more did he want?

Refusing to let himself even *think* about an answer to that, Lex sat at the piano and started to play, but he wasn't able to lose himself in the music the way he usually could, and when he heard the sound of the front door his hands paused above the keys and, in spite of everything he'd had to say to himself, his heart missed a beat as Romy appeared in the doorway.

Her dark hair was spangled with rain and she pushed it behind her ears with a stilted smile. 'I thought I heard the piano.'

'Where's Freya?' The constriction in Lex's chest made it hard to speak.

'Asleep in the hall.' Romy glanced over her shoulder. 'I've left her in the pushchair.'

There was a pause.

'I wasn't expecting you back yet,' he said at last.

'I didn't think *you'd* be back until later.'

'I decided to come home early.'

Romy moved into the room, hugging her arms together. 'Wasn't it a good weekend?'

'It was fine.' He shrugged. 'The usual.'

'How was your father?'

Lex made a face. 'Not so good. He seemed… tired.'

'Did you tell him about the deal?'

'Yes.'

'What did he say?'

'Nothing. He just looked away.'

Romy found herself clenching her fists on her sleeves. She knew Gerald Gibson was ill, but would it have been so hard for him to congratulate Lex, to somehow make it clear that he was proud of him?

'I'm sorry,' she said.

Lex pressed down a key with his forefinger, then another. 'I thought I would feel good about telling him,' he said abruptly. 'I thought I'd have proved something, but I just looked at him and realised that he didn't care. He's dying.'

'Oh, Lex.' Without thinking, Romy put her hands on his shoulders, and just for a moment Lex let himself lean back against her. Then he remembered that she was leaving and straightened.

'What about you? How did it go with Freya's father?'

'Fine.' Romy let her hands fall and moved away to the window, too restless to sit down. 'It was fine,' she said again. 'Michael was a bit stunned at first, understandably, but once he'd got used to the idea and met Freya he was quite chuffed. He said he'd like to get involved in her life.'

Lex raised his brows at her lack of enthusiasm.

'That's good news, isn't it? Most single mothers would welcome some support from the father.'

'I know.' With a sigh, Romy threw herself down on the sofa. 'I'm going to take Freya down again in a couple of weeks.'

'To stay with him?' Jealousy sharpened his voice, but she didn't seem to notice.

'No. Michael's back with his fiancée and they're getting married next year. Obviously he wants her to meet Freya, so I'll stay with Jenny again, and we'll have what I imagine will be quite an awkward get-together. But Michael seems to think Kate—that's his fiancée—will be OK about it once she meets me and sees I'm no threat.'

'And then what?' asked Lex harshly.

'What do you mean?'

'What happens once you've established a cosy relationship with this Michael and his oh-so-understanding fiancée?'

'I come back here and we see out this farce we've started,' said Romy. 'Jo should be back from maternity leave soon, and then I'll have to decide. I might move to Somerset. It's a lovely area, and it would be cheaper than London. And if Michael does want to see Freya regularly, that would work quite well.'

'Oh, I can see that would be the perfect set-up for you,' said Lex, bitterness threading his voice. 'Then you'd have everything you wanted, wouldn't you, Romy? Freya's father there for when you need him, but he's nicely tied up with his fiancée so there's no danger he'll try and get too close to you. No danger that you'll lose your precious independence!'

'You'll have everything *you* want too,' Romy

pointed out, caught unawares by the animosity that was suddenly crackling in the air. 'You'll have your precious deal and your nice, quiet life. What's the problem?'

'No problem.' Lex pushed back the piano stool and got abruptly to his feet. He was going out. He didn't know where. Just out. 'No problem at all.'

'Aren't you going out tonight?'

Lex was thrown when he let himself into his apartment the following Friday to find that Romy was sitting on the sofa with Freya, reading a story—or, rather, counting caterpillars while Freya smacked the pages. He had been coming home later and later that week, to avoid spending too much time with Romy, but that night he had expected her to be at the acquisition team's celebration dinner.

'I'm not going,' said Romy, looking up from the caterpillars. 'It's too difficult with Freya.'

Lex hung up his jacket and went back into the living room, frowning as he unbuttoned his cuffs and rolled up his sleeves. 'You should be there,' he said. 'You were an important part of the team, and if it hadn't been for you they might not have had anything to celebrate.'

Now he said it!

'It doesn't matter.' Romy managed a careless

shrug, hoping to conceal her disappointment. She really liked everyone in the team, and it promised to be a fun evening. They had all been dismayed when she said that she wouldn't be able to make it.

'I can't leave Freya,' she said. 'If I'd been at home, I could have asked my neighbour's daughter to babysit, but I don't know anyone I could trust around here.'

'You know me,' said Lex, and she stared at him, the book forgotten in her hands.

'I can't ask you to babysit!'

'Don't you trust me?'

'Of *course* I trust you, but… I couldn't ask you to do that.'

'I don't see why not,' Lex said. He sat down on the sofa opposite her and there was a squeak. Leaning to one side, he pulled out a much-chewed teddy bear.

Freya gave a cry of recognition and held out her hands for it.

'We've been looking for him,' said Romy as Lex leant over and handed the teddy back to Freya, who immediately stuffed its arm in her mouth.

'I'm just going to be here working,' he went on. 'As long as you put her to bed before you go, we'll be fine.'

'She doesn't usually wake up,' Romy agreed, weakening. It had been a long time since she'd been able to go out on her own, and she could already feel a lightening of her mood at the prospect. 'Are you sure you wouldn't mind?'

'If I minded, I wouldn't have offered,' said Lex brusquely.

So Romy got to go to the celebration dinner after all. Barely had the door closed behind her than Freya woke up. Lex tried to settle her in her cot, but nothing would console her, and in the end he succumbed and lifted her out. He had seen Romy walking her around, rubbing her back and humming soothingly, so he tried that, and it seemed to work.

Until he tried putting Freya back in her cot. She screamed and screamed and only stopped when Lex picked her up again and set off round the apartment once more.

Romy rang from the restaurant. 'Is everything all right?' she asked anxiously.

Lex was holding Freya in one arm, and the phone in his other hand. He craned his neck to peer at the baby, who was snuggled into his collar. Ridiculously long lashes, still damp with tears, lay across her flushed cheeks. She seemed to be all right. If he admitted that she'd been crying, Romy would come home and miss the dinner after all. There was no point in both of them listening to Freya cry.

'Everything's fine,' he said.

Lex didn't even get to open his briefcase that night. Freya categorically refused to go back into her cot and he spent the entire evening walking her round and round the flat. He hummed and he sang and he rocked her gently, and at last, worn out, he stretched out on the sofa and let Freya sprawl on his chest, where she promptly dropped into a deep slumber.

When Romy came back, she found them both sound asleep. Held securely by Lex's large hand, Freya lay flopped across his body, rising and falling with his chest.

Romy stood looking down at them, and her throat felt very tight. In sleep, Lex's stern features relaxed, and he looked younger and infinitely more approachable than when those piercingly pale eyes were open and he had himself under rigid control. The normally hard mouth was slightly ajar, and a soft whistling sound came out with every breath.

I don't want to fall in love with you, he had said. *I just don't want a baby.*

And yet he had looked after Freya all night, just so that Romy could go out and enjoy herself. Very lightly, she touched his hair.

Was she doing the right thing in running away from any thought of commitment? Romy wondered. It would be so easy to slip into a relationship. If she had said yes when Lex suggested that they continue to sleep together, she would have saved herself all the itchy, prickly, churning frustration of not being able to touch him. She would have been able to take it for granted that Lex would look after Freya when she went out. Romy had clung to her independence for so long, it was second nature to her now, but, still, there were times when even she could see how appealing it would be to have someone else to share the responsibility, someone else you could rely on utterly.

The trouble was, she could also see how painful it would be when that someone decided they didn't want to be with you any more. Romy's thoughts went round and round in familiar circles. She and Lex might be sexually compatible, but a relationship needed more than great sex. It needed more than Romy could give. It needed trust.

At one level, she trusted Lex completely. He would never betray her with another woman. He wasn't like her father, who had revelled in his double life. Lex had an almost old-fashioned sense of integrity. He might be short on the social skills in which his brother excelled but he was completely trustworthy in that sense.

No, Romy wasn't afraid he would leave her for another woman. What she feared was his inability to compromise. He would hate the mess and unpredictability of family life. He would hate not being able to control life with a baby, with a child, even with a woman.

And if he couldn't compromise, they couldn't live together, and they would split up. Romy wouldn't—*couldn't*—face being abandoned again. She couldn't trust that it wouldn't all go wrong and end in exactly the pain and mess that she was so determined Freya shouldn't suffer. She couldn't bear Freya to feel what she had felt when her father left.

No, better to keep her distance, Romy decided, and carry on as they were, but it was difficult to stay distant with Lex when they were living together. They walked into the office together in the morning, but after that first time he never again kissed her in Reception. Once there, they went their separate ways. Lex was far too senior for Romy to have any professional dealings with him. Rather to her surprise, her colleagues seemed to have accepted the idea of her being in a relationship with their chief executive.

'He's a behind-closed-doors kind of guy,' Romy had said to explain why Lex ignored her in the office. She wasn't sure whether the others believed her or not, but if they were baffled they kept any speculation to themselves.

It was surprising, too, how quickly she and Freya had adjusted to a completely new routine. Romy collected Freya from the crèche when it closed at five thirty and took her home. No, *not* home, she corrected herself and rewound her thoughts. She took Freya *back to Lex's flat*, gave her supper and a bath, and by then Lex was usually home.

Freya loved to sit on his lap at the piano while Romy tidied up the worst of the mess. Lex was stiff with her at first, but Freya was irresistible when she put her mind to it. Romy wondered if Lex realised how much he had changed. She liked to listen to him talking to Freya. He made no concessions to the fact that she was a baby, but talked to her as if she were an adult.

'That's F sharp,' he would say, pressing a key. 'And this one here is E. Now listen to this chord… And then if I do *this*, see what happens…'

Conversation wasn't a problem when Freya was around, but there was always a pool of silence once she was in bed. Occasionally Lex had some function to go to, but, if not, Romy usually prepared a meal for them to share.

'You don't need to cook for me,' Lex had protested, but Romy didn't like the prepared meals he was happy to cook straight from the freezer.

'I'm cooking for Freya anyway,' she said. 'Besides, I enjoy it.'

It was true, and it gave her something to do in the evenings. Something that wasn't remembering how sure, how warm, his hands had been. That wasn't reliving that night at Duncardie. Something that wasn't wishing that she had said yes instead of no, so that she could stand behind him and massage the tension from his neck and shoulders. If she could do that, she could press her mouth to his throat, trail kisses along his jaw until he turned his head to meet her lips with his own, let him pull her down onto his lap...

No, cooking was a much safer option.

CHAPTER NINE

AFTERWARDS she would pretend to read while Lex worked, but what Romy liked best was when he sat at the piano and forgot that she was there at all. During the day, he held himself rigid and guarded, shutting out the rest of the world, but at a piano his whole body seemed to relax and he swayed instinctively with the music while his fingers drew magic from the keys.

Her book would fall unheeded into her lap, and she would tip her head back and close her eyes. Romy had never had much of a feeling for music before, but when Lex played it felt as if he were strumming a chord deep inside her, and an intense *feeling* swelled in her chest and closed her throat.

'You should play professionally,' she said to him one night when he paused.

'I don't want to,' said Lex. 'And I don't have time. In case you haven't noticed, I've got a company to run.'

On the sofa, Romy tipped her head right back on the cushions until she could see him behind her. 'You could let Phin run the company.'

'Phin?' He gave a bark of laughter. 'Phin would give away all our assets and spend all our profits on staff development!' He was only half joking. 'Gibson & Grieve would never recover!'

'He's not as irresponsible as you think he is,' said Romy, leaping to the defence of her old friend. She and Phin had been close long before she had thought of Lex as anything more than Phin's intimidating older brother. 'Everyone I know thinks very highly of him.'

'Of course they do. Everyone likes Phin.' Resentment he hadn't even known he felt splintered Lex's voice. 'He's one of the most successful people I know. He goes his own sweet way, and because he makes people laugh, he gets away with it.

'Our father wanted him to join Gibson & Grieve when he left university, but you didn't catch Phin knuckling down and doing what he was supposed to do. Oh, no, Phin was off, drifting around the world, doing exactly what he wanted to do! He never cared about responsibility or the family or putting something back into the company that had paid for everything he had.'

Romy twisted right round so that she could look

at him over the back of the sofa. 'Is that what you've been doing all these years?'

'Someone had to.' Lex closed the piano lid. 'I was the eldest. I suppose it was inevitable that I was expected to be the sensible one. Phin just clapped me on the shoulder, told me not to let it get me down, and took off.' His mouth twisted in a humourless smile at the memory. 'My parents were beside themselves, but Phin didn't care.'

'He came back when your father had a stroke.'

'Yes, he did. He's the golden boy now that he's married Summer and settled down. Talk about the prodigal son!'

'You sound like you resent him,' said Romy carefully.

'I do, don't I?' Lex got to his feet and prowled over to the long, glass wall. He could see the lights along the Embankment and the dull gleam of the river.

'I think I envy him more than resent him,' he said at length. 'Everything seems to come easily to Phin. He's never cared half as much about our father's opinion as I do, but he's got his approval by doing exactly what he wanted.'

He turned back to face Romy. 'And I'll admit, he hasn't been quite such a disaster as a director as I feared he would be. Mind you, I think that's mostly down to Summer. Marrying her was the most sensible thing Phin ever did. But he hasn't got the dedication to run Gibson & Grieve, even if he wanted to.'

'There must be other directors who could take over as Chief Executive,' Romy pointed out. 'It's not as if you need the money.'

'It's not about money,' he said curtly.

'Then what *is* it about?'

Lex hunched a shoulder, wishing Romy would stop asking awkward questions. 'It's about my career. It's what I do. What I've always done. What I *am*. If you think I've spent my life wishing I could have been a musician instead of going into the family firm, forget it. Music is just…an escape.'

Romy looked up at him with her great dark eyes. 'Escape from what?' she asked softly.

Lex didn't answer immediately. He went back to the piano, laid his hand on the smooth mahogany. Even silent, he could feeling the piano's power strumming through the wood, calling to something inside him.

'We all make choices,' he said finally. 'I made mine, and I don't regret it. Do you regret any of the choices you've made?'

Romy thought about hot wind soughing through palm trees. About desert skies and coral reefs and drinking beer at a roadside *warung* while the tropical rain thundered down. And then she thought

about Freya and the friends she had made at
Gibson & Grieve and this crazy pretence she and
Lex were engaged in. She had chosen them all.

'No,' she said in low voice. 'The only choices I
regret are the ones that were made for me. I wasn't
allowed to choose whether my father stayed or
not, and nor was my mother. We just had to live
with the consequences of a choice *he* had made.'

She looked at Lex, still smoothing his hand
absently over the piano. 'I learnt from that,' she
said. 'I learnt to never give anyone else the power
to make a choice for me, and I never will.'

Freya was crying again. Lex squinted at the digital
display on the clock by his bed. Three seventeen.

She had been restless the night before as well.
Teething, Romy had said. This was the fifth time
he had heard Romy get up tonight, and Lex
couldn't stand it any more. Pulling on a pair of
trousers, he went to see if he could help.

Romy was walking Freya around the living
room, just as he had done the night she had gone
out to celebrate with the acquisitions team. She
was barefoot, and wearing a paisley-patterned
silk dressing gown that she had bought from a
charity shop. The merest glimpse of it was usually
enough to make Lex's body tighten with anticipation, imagining the slippery silk against her

skin, but tonight it was a mark of how exhausted Romy looked that his first thought was not what it would be like to pull at the belt and let the dressing gown slither from her shoulders, but to wonder how best he could help her.

He rubbed a tired hand over his face. 'Is there anything I can do?'

Romy felt as if there were lead weights attached to her eyelids. The effort of putting one foot in front of another was like wading through treacle. And yet it seemed there were enough hormones still alert enough to stir at the sight of Lex's lean, muscled body. His hair was rumpled, his jaw prickled with stubble, and the pale eyes shadowed with concern. She must look even worse than she felt, Romy realised. And that was saying something.

'I'm sorry—' she started but Lex interrupted her.

'Don't be sorry,' he said. 'Just tell me how I can help.' He moved closer, craning his neck to try and see Freya's face. 'What's the matter? Are you sure she's not sickening for anything?'

'No, she's just miserable with this tooth coming through. And I'm just miserable because I've got to go to Windsor for a meeting tomorrow with Tim,' she added wryly. 'Although I'm not sure how much use I'll be. I'll be lucky if I can string two words together.'

A frown touched Lex's eyes. 'In that case, why don't you let me take her while you try and get some sleep?'

Romy's body was craving sleep. The need to lie down and close her eyes was so strong that, instead of insisting that she could manage on her own as she would normally have done, she said only, 'But what about you?'

'I haven't got anything urgent on tomorrow—or today, I should say.' Lex jerked his head in the direction of her room. 'Go on, go back to bed. You won't be any good to Gibson & Grieve otherwise,' he said gruffly. 'If I can't manage, I'll wake you, I promise.'

To Romy's surprise, Freya allowed herself to be handed over to Lex without a murmur. She subsided, sniffling, into his bare shoulder, and for one appalling moment Romy actually found herself thinking, *Lucky Freya*. She must be more tired than she thought she was.

She managed four hours' sleep and felt almost human when she woke. Freya was quieter than normal, but she seemed better, so in the end Romy decided to leave her in the crèche and headed off to Windsor with Tim. They were due back by four. Freya ought to be OK until then, she tried to reassure herself.

'But ring me if there's a problem,' she told the

girls in the crèche, who promised they would. They were used to anxious mothers.

Up in the chief executive's office, Lex was also feeling the results of a broken night. His eyes were gritty and there seemed to be a tight band snapped around his skull. He was distracted all morning.

'What?' he snapped at Summer when he caught her watching him narrowly.

'I was just wondering if you were feeling all right,' said Summer, who wasn't in the least frightened of him. 'You're not yourself today.'

'I'm fine,' he said shortly. 'I didn't get much sleep last night, that's all.'

When she had gone back to her office, Lex took off his glasses and sat rubbing the bridge of his nose. He was thinking about Freya. She had barely slept all night. Romy seemed sure teething was the problem, but what if it was something else? What if she needed a doctor? The crèche presumably had lots of children to deal with. Would anyone notice if she wasn't well?

He glanced at his watch. Romy would still be in Windsor.

On an impulse, he leant forward and buzzed Summer. 'Where's this crèche we provide?'

'On the mezzanine.' Summer didn't even seem surprised by the question.

'I'm just going to have a look,' Lex said on his

way out, and then wondered why he was making excuses to his PA.

He would just go and check that Freya was all right, he decided. And then perhaps he could get on with some work.

The crèche manager, flustered by the unannounced arrival of the chief executive, showed him round. The room was full of small children and babies, and the noise was indescribable. Amongst all the tiny tables and chairs, Lex felt like a clumsy giant who had stumbled into a world on quite a different scale. He picked his way carefully across the room, terrified of treading on something.

Freya was being comforted by one of the staff in a quiet corner and looking very woebegone. She had clearly been grizzling but offered a wobbly smile when she saw Lex and held out her arms to him. The girl exchanged looks with the manager as the chief executive took the baby and let her clutch his hair.

'She doesn't seem very happy,' he said severely.

'We've just rung her mother to say that Freya's a little poorly today. She's on her way back.'

Lex frowned. 'It might take her some time to get back from Windsor.'

'Yes, she said it would be a while, but we'll keep Freya here. She'll be fine,' the manager reassured him.

'As long as she's all right.' Lex tried to hand Freya back then, but she wailed in protest and clung to him until the manager prised her off him.

Feeling like a traitor, Lex headed for the door. Freya's heartbroken screams followed him until he couldn't stand it any more. Stopping abruptly, he pulled out his mobile phone and rang Romy.

'How long will it take you to get back?' he asked.

'I'm waiting for a train now. I'll get a taxi when I get to Paddington, but I'll still be about an hour, I think.' Romy's voice was riddled with guilt. 'I shouldn't have left her.'

'The manager says that she's fine, but it's pretty noisy in there,' said Lex. 'Shall I take her to my office? It'll be quieter there.'

Romy was silent. He could almost hear her instinct not to rely on anyone else warring with her concern for her daughter. In the end, Freya won, as Lex had known she would. Romy spoke to the manager on his mobile, and the moment Lex took her back Freya's screams subsided. They faded to shuddery little gasps as he waited for the lift.

There were three other people already in the lift when the doors opened. After a startled glance at Lex and his unusual burden, they all kept their eyes studiously on the floor numbers as they lit up one by one, but Lex was sure that behind his back they were exchanging looks. In a matter of minutes, the word would have spread around the building that the chief executive had been spotted in a lift with a baby in one arm , a bright yellow bag sporting teddy bears over the other, and a pushchair in his spare hand.

If Summer was surprised to see Lex reappear with a baby, she gave no sign of it. Coming round her desk, she tickled Freya's nose, and Freya managed a very little smile for her, but refused to be handed over or put down. Lex ended up dictating as he paced around the office while Summer wisely kept her inevitable reflections to herself.

Eventually, Freya dropped off, worn out. Lex wished he could do the same. He tilted the pushchair back as far as it would go and was laying her carefully in it when the phone rang.

'That was Romy.' Summer put the phone down. 'Apparently there's some delay on the line. She doesn't know when she'll be able to get here now. She sounded frantic, but I told her not to worry, that Freya was fine and sleeping.'

'Yes, it's all right for some, isn't it?' Lex straightened the blanket over Freya, caught Summer's eye and stood hastily. 'Well, perhaps now we can get on with some work,' he said brusquely.

Summer smiled. 'Perhaps,' she agreed. 'You haven't forgotten you've got a meeting at four-thirty, have you?'

Lex slapped a hand to his forehead. 'God, yes! I had forgotten.'

What was happening to him? He *never* forgot meetings. He knew Summer was thinking exactly the same thing.

'Let's just hope she stays asleep,' he said, looking down at Freya dubiously.

He might have spared his breath. She woke up, bang on time, a minute before the meeting was due to start, all smiles and apparently miraculously cured. She was ready for some attention, she indicated, and had no intention of being left out of the action. When Lex left her with Summer to join the directors waiting in his office, Freya's bellows of outrage could be heard clearly through the wall.

Lex put his head back round the door. 'Can't you keep her quiet?' he demanded irritably.

'No,' said Summer, not mincing her words. 'She doesn't want to be with me. She wants to be with you.'

So Lex had to conduct the meeting with Freya tweaking his nose or tugging at his ear lobes. It was hard to look intimidating with a baby on your lap.

That was what was left of his reputation shot to pieces, thought Lex in resignation.

It was almost half past five before Romy got there, looking hot and frazzled. 'Oh, thank God!'

she said as she swept up a smiling Freya and kissed her. 'I've been so worried. How has she been?'

'Absolutely fine,' said Summer. 'In fact, I'm thinking of taking her on as an assistant. She had all those men in suits terrified. They were in and out of that meeting in double quick time!' She slid an amused glance in Lex's direction. 'And she can run rings around our chief executive!'

'I thought she wasn't well,' Lex said defensively.

'It was quite a revelation. I'd no idea you were so good with babies.' Summer's eyes twinkled. 'I can't wait to tell Phin!'

'God, I'll never hear the end of it once Phin knows,' Lex grumbled as he walked Romy and Freya to the lift.

The afternoon might have been designed to prove that work and children didn't mix. Between lack of sleep and having to drop everything the moment a child was ill, it was impossible to get any work done. He was just glad he didn't have to deal with crises like this one on a regular basis.

'I'm sorry Freya threw out your afternoon, but I'm so grateful,' said Romy. 'I don't know what I'd have done without you.'

He hunched a shoulder. 'I dare say she'd have been all right in the crèche.'

'Yes, but she was much happier with you.'

Romy pushed Freya back to the apartment,

feeling deeply uneasy. Yes, she was grateful that
Lex had been able to help, but it was disturbing to
realise just how comfortable Freya was with him.
He wasn't supposed to be important to her. That
was exactly what Romy hadn't wanted to happen.

She was going to have to do something about
it, and soon.

'Is there any news of the contract?' she asked Lex
that night as she wiped down Freya's high chair.

'There is.' Lex had almost forgotten about it in
all the anxiety about Freya. 'Everything's going
ahead much quicker than we thought. Summer
has been in touch with Willie's assistant, and
they're trying to arrange the formal signing at the
end of next week.'

'Next week!' Romy was horrified at the way her
heart leapt in dismay. She was supposed to be
looking forward to ending this awkward situation
and moving on. Hadn't she decided that things
needed to change soon? It was just that she hadn't
counted on them changing quite that soon.

She summoned a smile. 'Well, that's great news.'

'Yes,' said Lex, then, thinking that sounded a bit
bald, 'Yes, it is.'

Romy stashed the chair in the corner and began
to pull the waxed cloth off the table. 'I'll be able
to make some plans now.'

'What sort of plans?'

'About the future. I had time to think while I was stuck on that train today, and I've realised I can't go on like this.' She concentrated on folding the cloth neatly. Lex hated it when she just scrumpled it up and tossed it on the floor beside the high chair. 'Tim offered me a permanent job today,' she told Lex, who stilled. 'But I've decided not to take it.'

When she glanced at Lex, she saw that his brows were drawn together. 'Why not?'

'Because it's too difficult being in London. Luckily you were there to take Freya today, but what if she was unwell another time and I couldn't get to her in time?'

'I could always help,' Lex offered stiffly, but Romy shook her head.

'I couldn't ask you to do that again. You're Chief Executive, and I know how busy you are. You've got more important things to do.' She drew a breath. 'No, I've decided I'm going to move to Somerset. If I live near Michael, at least he'd be able to help if necessary.'

She and Freya had met Kate, Michael's fiancée, the previous weekend. She had seemed very nice, and if she resented the fact that Michael had been suddenly thrust into fatherhood, she didn't show it.

'Jenny's down there, too,' Romy went on. 'She

said she'd be happy for me to stay until I find a job
and a place of my own.'

It made sense, Lex told himself as he lay in bed
and tried to ignore the weight pressing on his
chest. And not just for Romy. Once she and Freya
had gone, life would go back to normal.

He was sick of the edginess that churned con-
tinually in the pit of his stomach. He was tired of
the way his lungs tightened whenever he caught
sight of Romy in the morning, looking sleepy and
rumpled and gorgeous. He had had enough of the
painful grip on his heart, and the way it squeezed
every time she smiled. It was a ridiculous way for
a grown man to feel.

He was glad Willie Grant was coming soon, so
they could end this absurd charade. He had
already ruined his reputation because of it, Lex
reminded himself sourly. The whole company
would be talking about him carrying a baby in the
lift, and if he hadn't wanted to make it seem as if
he cared he would have asked the directors at the
meeting to keep quiet about the fact that he had
conducted an entire meeting while Freya tugged
at his lips and bumped her head against his.

What had he been thinking? It was as if he
had taken leave of his senses since Romy had
reappeared.

Well, that would end soon. She would leave, and

take Freya with her. Let her set up house near her
artist, if that was what she wanted. Lex imagined
Michael dropping by to see his daughter every
day. Freya would have him wound round her little
finger in no time. Michael would be the one she
held out her arms for. The one she flirted with and
played with and wanted when she was teething.

Lex's jaw set. And that was as it should be.
Michael was her father. He would be able to make
her happy in a way he, Lex, never could. How
could he be a father? He knew nothing about
relaxing or laughing or playing. The thought of
being responsible for anyone else's happiness
made him recoil. He wouldn't know where to
begin, and he didn't want to.

No, better that Romy took Freya away as soon
as possible.

It was all for the best.

'That was a fine meal,' said Willie, leaning back
in his chair and patting his stomach appreciatively.
'If only all business dinners were as good. You're
a grand cook, Romy. And, Lex, you're a very
lucky man!'

Lex's smile was brief. 'I know,' he said. He
didn't look at Romy.

Willie's visit was going exactly as planned.
Willie himself was in high good humour, as well

he might be, Lex reflected. He had been delighted to come to the apartment and Freya had been on her best behaviour with him before she went to bed. Romy had remembered that Willie's favourite food was lamb, and she'd roasted a leg with a herby crust. Lex had handed over a staggering amount of money for a bottle of Willie's favourite whisky.

Rarely had a major business deal taken place in such a cordial atmosphere. There was no question of Willie changing his mind now. Everything was perfect.

So why was Lex's stomach knotted with unease? Why was there this uncomfortable feeling between his shoulders?

Realising that the smile had dropped from his face, Lex put it back and forced his attention back to Willie, who was telling Romy about his marriage.

'Moira and I were together forty-seven years. She was a wonderful woman. Not everyone gets as lucky as you and I, Lex,' he added with a twinkling look. 'You're clearly a man who was prepared to do whatever it took to hang onto a good woman when you found her.'

And that was when Lex realised that he couldn't go through with it.

'Willie,' he said. 'There's something I have to tell you.'

'Oh?' Willie's smile faded and he put down his glass. 'That sounds serious.'

'It is.' Lex swallowed. 'I've brought you here under false pretences.'

Romy drew a startled breath and he held up a hand to stop her protest, keeping his eyes steadily on Willie.

'Romy and I aren't a couple, Willie, and we don't normally live together. This is nothing to do with Romy,' he added. 'When we realised that you thought we were a couple, it seemed important to you, and I saw a chance to persuade you to sign.'

'Actually, it was my idea,' Romy tried to put in, but Lex overrode her.

'It was my responsibility,' he said firmly. 'I told Romy I'd do anything to make this deal, but I should have drawn the line at lying.'

After the first moment of surprise, Willie's eyes had narrowed, but he said nothing, just watched Lex, who found himself trying to loosen his tie that all at once felt too tight.

'I'm sorry,' he said. 'I should have confessed all this before, and given you the chance to change your mind about the deal. You still can, of course.'

There was dead silence round the table. Willie looked from Lex to Romy and then back to Lex.

'Why are you telling me this now?' he asked at last.

Lex, who had braced himself for anger or disgust or disappointment, was thrown by the mildness of Willie's tone.

'I think the deal will be a good one for both our companies,' he said carefully after a moment. 'It's one I've wanted for a long time, and I thought I would do anything to make it happen, but...'

He stopped, tried to gather his thoughts. 'Before, you were just the owner of a chain of stores. I had respect for your business acumen, but I didn't know you. Now I do, and I've realised that your opinion matters to me.' Lex sounded almost surprised. 'Now I respect you as a person, and going ahead with this deal while effectively lying to you isn't respecting you. I don't want to do it.'

'I see,' said Willie thoughtfully. 'So you're telling me you don't love Romy?'

Lex hesitated. 'I'm telling you we're not a couple.'

Willie turned to Romy. 'And you don't love Lex?' he asked, sounding genuinely interested, and she bit her lip.

'I'm so sorry, Willie. We've just been pretending all this while.'

'Well.' Willie sat back in his chair, shaking his head in disbelief. 'You're not a real couple?'

'No.'

'Why not?'

There was a short silence. 'I'm sorry?' said Lex.

'Why *aren't* you a couple?' Willie said, all reasonableness. 'It seems to me that you're good together, and I notice you both avoided a direct answer when I asked about love.'

Romy glanced at Lex. 'Love isn't the problem,' she said in a low voice.

'Then what is?'

She couldn't tell Willie how her father had swept her up into his arms and called her his best girl, and abandoned her the next day. How could she explain how hard it was to trust when the man you loved most in the world, the man you trusted above all others, let you down? How could she tell him about Lex, who strove for his father's approval and kept his world under tight control?

'It's…complicated,' she said.

'What's complicated about loving each other?'

'I think Romy's trying to explain that we're incompatible,' Lex tried. This was the most bizarre business conversation he had ever had, but he supposed it was his fault for raising the matter in the first place.

Willie raised a sceptical brow. 'Is that right? I seem to remember seeing you two walking in the snow at Duncardie and you looked pretty compatible then.'

The colour rose in Romy's cheeks and Lex set his teeth. 'We just…want different things.'

'Haven't either of you heard of compromise? A fine pair of cowards you both are!'

Willie shook his head and pushed back his chair. 'I can't say I'm not disappointed,' he said, 'but it's not the first disappointment of my life and I dare say it won't be the last. Ah, well.' He hoisted himself upright. 'That was still a delicious dinner, Romy, so thank you for that—and for an interesting evening all round.'

Lex and Romy exchanged a glance, and Lex got to his feet. A limousine would be waiting below to take Willie back to his hotel. 'I'll see you to the car.'

'I didn't have you down for a fool, Alexander Gibson,' said Willie in the lift down to the basement garage, 'but I've changed my mind!'

'I can only apologise again,' Lex said stiffly. 'I wanted to make the deal so much, I let it override my judgement. I accept that it was a mistake.'

'Well, I've made some mistakes in my own time,' Willie allowed. 'I've tried to learn from them, and I hope you will too. What you learn, of course, is up to you.' He clapped Lex on the shoulder as they stepped out of the lift to see the limousine waiting. 'I'll see you tomorrow.'

'You mean you'll still sign?' Lex hardly dared believe that it would be all right.

'Oh, yes. You're right about it being a good thing for both companies.' His shrewd blue eyes rested on Lex's face. 'It's a funny thing,' he said, 'how you can feel disappointed in someone and yet proud of them at the same time. I've been watching what you've done for Gibson & Grieve, laddie. You've moved into a whole new league, and you've got yourself a fine reputation. If you hadn't, I would never have agreed to sell, no matter how married you were.

'And knowing how much this deal matters to you means I can appreciate what it took for you to tell me the truth,' he said. 'It was the right thing to do, and I'm glad you did it. So I'm proud of you, and I'll be happy to sign that contract tomorrow.'

He smiled at Lex as they shook hands. 'But that doesn't mean I don't still think you're a fool when it comes to Romy!'

Romy was clearing the table when Lex let himself back into the flat. She looked up, her hands full of plates, but put them back on the table when she saw his face.

'So, no more pretending,' she said.

'No.' Lex dropped his keys onto the side table.

'Why did you tell him, Lex?'

'I had to.'

Loosening his tie, he went over to the window and stood looking down at the river. The lights along the Embankment were blurry in the drizzle, and he thought about Willie, driving back alone to his hotel.

He turned to look at Romy, who was wiping her hands on a tea towel and watching him with dark, wary eyes.

'He's going to sign anyway.'

Romy's shoulders slumped with relief. 'I thought he'd be furious that we'd been lying to him.'

'He told me I was a fool,' said Lex. 'But he also understood what I've been trying to do with Gibson & Grieve. He said he was proud of me.' Ashamed of the strain in his voice, he looked back at the view. 'Do you know how long I've waited for my own father to say that?'

Dropping the tea towel over the back of a chair, Romy went over to stand beside him. 'Just because he hasn't said it, doesn't mean he doesn't think it, Lex. If Willie can appreciate what you've done for Gibson & Grieve, then your father must be able to as well. It's just more difficult for him to accept that he wasn't indispensable, and that the company is moving on without him. You know that,' she said gently.

'Yes, I know that.' Lex's expression was bleak. For a while they stood side by side, looking out across the lights of London. Then he let out a long breath, letting the old frustration go.

He glanced at Romy, then away again. 'What did you mean when you told Willie that love wasn't the problem?'

'It isn't,' she said. 'The problem is that love doesn't last. The problem is that it isn't enough.'

'Willie thinks it is. It lasted forty-seven years for him and Moira.'

'They were lucky,' said Romy. 'We might not be.' She turned restlessly, rubbing her arms. 'It's all very well for Willie to say compromise, but how would that actually work? Do you *really* want to give up your tidy flat and your nice, ordered life?'

'We could compromise in other ways,' Lex suggested.

'How? A flat like this isn't suitable for a toddler.' She gestured around her. 'How long before I get fed up with all the sharp angles and slippy floors? Before I start resenting the fact that there's no garden or other children nearby? Before I think that if I have to manoeuvre that pushchair into the lift one more time I'm going to scream?

'And how long before you're gritting your teeth about the mess? Until you're exasperated by the chaos and the noise and disgusted by the dirty nappies and Freya's runny nose?'

Romy shook her head. 'Compromise is hard, Lex. And I can't take the risk that you'll be able to do it. If it was just me, then perhaps. But I've got Freya to think about too. When you've got a child, you have to put practicalities before passion. I have to think about Freya and what she needs. She'd be better off in the country, where I can afford to give her a better life.

'It would be so easy to stay here with you,' she said. 'To think, oh, well, let's give it a go, but you said it yourself: we're different, and we want different things. I don't see how it could work, and if we try and it doesn't work it'll hurt all of us.'

Lex was watching her pace fretfully to and fro, her arms hugged together.

'So you're saying that you love me, but you don't love me enough to be sure it would work out?'

Romy lifted her chin. 'Do you love me enough to put up with all the mess and uncertainty that comes from living with a child?'

Fatally, Lex hesitated, and she smiled sadly. 'I didn't think so.'

'I think it might be worth a try,' he insisted, but she shook her head.

'I can't take that risk, Lex. I don't dare.'

She drew a breath, let it out shakily. 'Freya and I will go back to my flat tomorrow,' she said. 'Jo's back next week, so the maternity cover finishes then. I'm going to move down to Somerset straight away.'

'And what do we tell all those people who are now convinced that we're having a raging affair?'

'Tell them it didn't work out,' said Romy. 'For once, we won't have to pretend.'

CHAPTER TEN

'I THINK that's everything.' Lex set down the high chair and the changing mat. The hallway of Romy's tiny flat was crammed with bags and baby equipment.

It had been a long day. They had both gone to the signing ceremony, and had smiled and smiled for the inevitable photographs. Then they had said goodbye to Willie Grant, who told them to get in touch when they'd come to their senses. And after that there had been nothing to do but to collect up all Romy's stuff from the flat, and Lex had driven them home.

Except it didn't feel like home any more. The flat was cold and poky and dreary and Romy's throat was so tight she could hardly speak. Any moment now, she was going to have to say goodbye to Lex, and she didn't know how she was going to bear it.

He looked all wrong in this shabby flat.

Freya was sitting on the floor of the living

room, puzzled by suddenly finding herself somewhere new. She looked around doubtfully as if not at all sure what she was doing there. Romy knew how she felt.

'Will I see you before you go?' Lex asked at last, and she drew a breath to steady herself.

'I think it's probably easier if we don't.'

His eyes shuttered. 'Perhaps you're right.'

The silence was excruciating.

'Well.' Romy lifted her hands and let them drop. 'I…er…I should probably give Freya her tea.'

'Yes. I'll go.'

Lex squatted down next to Freya and smoothed down the absurd quiff of hair. She looked up at him with those round, astounded eyes, her face dissolving into a smile, and the cold stone where Lex's heart had once been splintered into shards. 'Be good,' he said, and straightened before his voice could crack.

Romy was waiting by the door. Her dark eyes were shimmering with unshed tears.

'I don't know how to say goodbye,' she confessed.

'Then don't,' said Lex. He put his hands on her arms and wondered if this was the last time he would see her for another twelve years. 'I love you,' he said. 'I've always loved you.'

'And I love you.' Romy was desperately blinking back the tears, but it was a losing battle.

'I do,' she insisted as if he hadn't believed her. 'I just wish…'

She wished it were enough, but it wasn't.

'I know,' said Lex, and, because there wasn't any other way to say goodbye, he smoothed his hands up over her shoulders and up her throat to cradle her jaw. 'I just wish too,' he said, and kissed her.

Romy leant into him, slipping her arms around his waist to hold him close, and they kissed, a fierce, desperate kiss that said everything words couldn't.

This will be the last time, Romy thought, even as her senses spun. The last time I touch him. The last time he kisses me. The last time I feel as if I'm exactly where I'm meant to be.

Even as she tried to hold onto the sensation, Lex was giving her one last, longing kiss and dropping his hands. He stepped back and reached for the door. Opened it.

Romy was standing exactly where he had left her, her mouth pressed in a straight line to stop it shaking, and her eyes dark and dazed.

Unable to resist one last touch, Lex wiped a tear from her cheek with his thumb. 'Goodbye, Romy,' he said gently, and then he was gone.

The phone was ringing as Romy manoeuvred the pushchair into the narrow cottage hall and shut the door behind her. Keys still clenched between her teeth, she ran into the kitchen to grab the cordless phone, only just remembering to spit out the keys in time.

'Hello?' she said breathlessly.

'Romy? It's Mum. I'm afraid I've got some sad news.'

Gerald Gibson was dead. 'Another stroke,' Molly told Romy. 'A merciful release in some ways, but of course Faith is devastated. He wasn't an easy man, but she adored him and she feels so alone now. She's got Lex and Phin, I know, but it's not the same. She and Gerald loved each other so much, I often thought those boys missed out.'

The funeral was to be the following Friday. 'You should be there for Faith,' her mother said. 'She's your godmother. And Phin was always a good friend to you, wasn't he?'

And Lex, Romy wanted to cry. Lex mattered most of all.

She had been in Somerset for seven weeks, and everything had fallen into place as if it were meant to be. She had found a little cottage in the same village as Jenny. It was a bit like living in a doll's house, with tiny rooms and a handkerchief garden, but it was enough for Freya. If Romy sometimes felt as if she couldn't breathe, and thought longingly of Lex's spacious apartment, well, that was a price of independence and she was happy to pay it.

Michael lived nearby, but not too close, and he and Kate had taken Freya for the afternoon a few times now. She hadn't spent the night with them yet, but Romy had no doubt that would come. Michael was making the effort to get to know his daughter, and that could only be a good thing. He had offered Romy financial support, but she had suggested that he invest the money for Freya instead. A relationship between Freya and her father was one thing. Accepting money was quite another. Money would be a tie. Romy wasn't ready for that.

She had found a job. Only part-time for now, but it was a start. People in the village were friendly. They could live cheaply. She ought to be happy, Romy reminded herself. She had everything she needed.

Except Lex.

Time and again, Romy assured herself that she had made the right decision. She and Freya couldn't have stayed in the apartment. They would have driven Lex mad. Much better to have made the break now, before either of them had a chance to be hurt.

It didn't feel better though. There was a dull ache inside her, all the time, like a weight pressing on her heart, and misery clogged her throat so that speaking was an effort and even swallowing hurt.

In spite of the claustrophobically cluttered rooms in the cottage, it felt as if something was missing, and it took Romy a little time to accept that she was constantly looking round, hoping to see Lex. She wanted to see him peering over the top of his reading glasses or tugging at the knot of his tie. She wanted to see the stern mouth relaxing into a smile as he picked up Freya, or holding the tiny hands between his large ones as he helped her to play the piano.

Always in the past Romy had been able to move on without a backward glance, but this time it was different. She missed London more than she thought she would. She had always liked wild, exotic places, but now she missed the buzz of work and the banter with her colleagues. She missed standing at Lex's window and looking down at the great city spread out below.

She missed Lex most of all.

Freya missed him, too, Romy was sure. She couldn't say so, but she was lacklustre and fretful. Romy knew exactly how she felt. For the first time in her life, she was lonely. Oh, Freya was there, and she could always pop round to see Jenny, but it wasn't the same as living with Lex. There was no one to tell when Freya learnt another word, no one to laugh when she put her pants on her head. No one to say hello to in the morning.

No one to make her heart leap at the sound of the key in the door.

She wanted to tell him when Freya took her first step. She'd told her mother, she'd told Jenny, she'd even told Michael, but the person she really wanted to tell was Lex. She even picked up the phone and got as far as dialling his mobile before she cut the connection.

What was the point of calling him?

She would hear his voice and he would hear hers, but wouldn't that just make it worse? And after Lex had said, 'Great news,' or whatever you said when a baby took their first step, what then? What would there be left to talk about? She and Lex couldn't be friends—they were too close for that—but they couldn't be lovers either. She should leave him to get on with his life, and get on with her own.

But now the father Lex had tried so hard to please was dead, and Romy wished desperately that she could have been there for him when he needed her.

Except Lex hadn't wanted her there, she reminded herself. If he had, he would have phoned and told her himself, instead of letting her hear it from her mother. Perhaps, like her, he had decided that in the end it would just make it harder. So Romy didn't ring him either, but wrote a short note that said everything that was proper about his father and nothing at all about what she really wanted to say.

That Friday she left Freya with Michael, and made her way to Gloucestershire. The funeral was to be held in the village where Lex's parents had lived for forty years. A car was beyond Romy's budget, so it was a complicated journey involving buses, trains and taxis, and she only just made it to the church in time for the service.

Her mother, so long a friend to Faith Gibson, was sitting behind the family. Romy slipped into the end of the pew, exchanging a glance of apology for her lateness with her mother.

In front of her, Faith sat between her two sons. Summer was there, too, sitting next to Phin. They were a family, and yet Lex looked alone. He was staring straight ahead. Something about the rigid set of his shoulders, the careful way he held his head, twisted Romy's heart. He was suffering, and there was nothing she could do to help.

The organ struck up, and the priest was moving to address the congregation. Romy saw Lex brace himself, and without giving herself time to think she got up and slid into the pew in front. He shouldn't have to be on his own, not today.

She caught Lex unawares. The vicar had already begun the service, so there was no chance to talk, but Romy saw the startled look in his eyes change to a fierce gladness, and when she took his hand his fingers closed around hers hard. He didn't say anything and he didn't look at her again, but he held her hand tightly all through the service, only letting her go when he got up to give the eulogy.

After the service, Romy stepped back, still without a word, and let Lex take his mother to the graveside, while her own mother eyed her speculatively.

'Is there something I should know?' she asked after the burial was over and they were walking slowly to the Gibsons' house behind the family. It was an inappropriately beautiful day, and the village was so small no one had thought to get in a car to drive the short distance from the church to the house.

Romy flushed under her mother's scrutiny. She had acted on impulse, and she was glad that she had, but to her mother it must have looked odd the way she had pushed into the family pew.

'I didn't want Lex to be on his own.'

Incredibly, neither her mother nor Faith Gibson seemed to have heard anything about the time she and Freya had spent with Lex. Summer had certainly known that they were living together, which meant that Phin must have known too, but evidently he hadn't passed the news on around the family. Romy wondered whether this was tact on his part, or if Lex had asked him not to say anything.

As far as Romy's mother knew, Lex was no more than a family friend to Romy. Someone you bumped into at weddings and funerals like this. She knew nothing about that crazy week in Paris all those years ago. She had no idea that Lex knew Freya or that he made her daughter's heart turn over just by walking into the room.

But Romy had had enough pretending, she realised. 'I'm in love with Lex,' she told her mother abruptly, and it was a huge relief just to say the words.

Molly's eyes rounded and for a moment she looked exactly like Freya. 'With *Lex*? But how…? When…?' She shook her head to clear it. 'Why didn't you tell me?' And then, unable to help herself, 'Does Faith know?'

'I don't think so.'

'But, darling, this is wonderful news!' In deference to the other mourners, Molly kept her voice down, but she couldn't resist giving Romy a hug. 'Why the big secret? And why move to Somerset? I thought you wanted to get back together with Freya's father!'

'No.' Romy's steps slowed. She was remembering all the reasons why going to Somerset had seemed such a good idea. Was *still* a sensible idea. 'I just wanted to get away from Lex. I don't want to love him, Mum. You know what Lex is like. We're too different. Anyway,' she said, 'we agreed it wouldn't work.'

'Ah.' Her mother's gaze rested thoughtfully on Romy's face. 'Does Lex love you?'

'I think he loves me, yes.' Romy sighed. 'That isn't the problem,' she said, just as she had to Willie Grant. 'What if love isn't enough? What if it doesn't last? You and Dad loved each other, and look what happened to you!'

'Oh, Romy,' said her mother a little helplessly. 'Yes, I loved your father, but it wasn't all perfect. It takes two to make a marriage, and two to let a relationship break down. I know how much it hurt you when he left, but I'm not sure it would have been better for you if he'd stayed. Would you really have wanted to have grown up in a home where the adults resent each other, knowing that you were the only reason they stayed together? I don't think so.'

Romy stopped at that and stared at her mother. 'Are you saying you think it was a good thing that he left us?'

'No, never that. Not knowing what it did to you. But it wasn't actually the end of the world, was it?' Molly took her daughter's arm and made her keep walking. 'I was very unhappy for a time, but then I met Keith, and I'm happier being married to him than I ever was with your father. I don't have any regrets about marrying Tony, though. We had you, didn't we? How could either of us regret that? And now I can remember the good times.'

She smiled at her daughter. 'There are no guarantees when it comes to love, Romy. Maybe it won't work out with Lex, but maybe it will, and if you never take the risk, you'll never know how happy you could be.'

Lex's jaw felt rigid but he kept a smile in place as he went to greet his godmother. He had always been fond of Molly, who had luminous dark eyes just like her daughter's, but he had been avoiding her, just as he had been avoiding thinking about Romy, who stood now by her mother's side.

He had been feeling so alone in the church, and then suddenly Romy had been there. The feel of her hand in his had been so comforting that Lex had almost convinced himself that he had made it up. His mother had been too bound up in her own grief to notice anything, and Romy had slipped away when they followed the coffin out to the graveside. It was almost as if she had never been there at all.

But he had seen her as soon as she came into the house with Molly, and he had spent the afternoon torn between joy at her presence and despair that he was going to have to get used to her not being there all over again. He hadn't talked to her. He didn't know what he would say. The only thing he could think of to say was, 'Come back, I miss you,' but what was the point? Romy had made her choice, and he had to live with it. Better not to say anything at all.

So Lex moved through the afternoon like an automaton, talking to guests, agreeing that they would all miss his father, not letting himself think. Especially not letting himself notice Romy, slender and vibrant in the dark suit she had used to wear to work. Today she had substituted a dark purple top for her usual brightly coloured blouses, but she still looked more vivid than anyone else in the room.

She was a flame, constantly catching at the edge of his vision. It didn't matter that she was only talking quietly to other guests. She spoke to his mother, to Phin and Summer. She did nothing to draw attention to herself at all, but Lex was intensely aware of her all the same. She might as well have been the only other person in the room.

Now Lex kissed Molly's cheek, and let himself look properly at Romy at last. She looked gravely back at him, her eyes dark and warm, and as his gaze met hers there was such a rightness to it, as if everything were suddenly falling into place, that Lex was sure that everyone in the room must surely hear the click of connection.

His jaw was clenched so tightly he could feel the tendons standing out in his neck. 'Thank you for coming,' he said.

There, he hadn't seized her in his arms. He hadn't humiliated himself by begging her to come home. It wasn't much of a victory, but Lex felt as if he had negotiated a long and arduous obstacle course.

'Faith looks all in,' said Molly, apparently not noticing the way her daughter and Lex were staring desperately at each other.

With difficulty, he dragged his eyes from Romy's. 'Yes. Yes, she is. Phin and Summer are going to take her home with them.'

'And you?'

'I'm going back to London too.'

'On your own?'

'Yes,' said Lex, unable to keep the bleakness from his voice. 'On my own.'

There was a pause. 'I think I'll go and say goodbye to Faith,' said Molly.

Lex was left alone with Romy. The moment he had longed for. The moment he had dreaded.

Romy drew a breath. 'Can I come with you?' she said.

'Where?'

'To London.'

The dark eyes were drawing him in. Lex could feel himself slipping. Any moment now and he would be falling again, tumbling wildly out of control once more. He made himself look away.

'I think I need to be on my own,' he said.

Romy put her hand on his arm. 'No, you need someone with you,' she told him gently.

'Romy, I can't…' Lex broke off, groped for control. 'I can't say goodbye again.'

'We're not going to say goodbye.'

Mutely, he shook his head, and Romy shattered what was left of his defences by stepping closer so that his senses reeled with her nearness, with the warmth of her hand, the piercing familiarity of her fragrance.

'Lex, you buried your father today,' she said. 'I know you've been strong for your mother, but you need to grieve for yourself. Now let me be strong for you. Let me drive you. You don't have to do everything on your own.'

The longing to be with her, to put off the moment when he had to watch her leave, was too much. Strong? He had never been strong where she was concerned. Lex did his best to resist the temptation, but then handed over his car keys. It felt deeply symbolic. He wanted to say, 'Be careful, that's my heart I'm giving you there.'

He didn't, of course, but Romy smiled reassuringly at him anyway. 'Don't worry,' she said. 'I'm a careful driver.'

Lex was used to being driven. He often sat in the back of limousines, but this was different. He was sitting in the passenger seat of his own car, and Romy was at the wheel, and he was very aware of having ceded control. It felt dangerous. And it felt like letting go.

Letting go of responsibility.

Letting go of the pretence that he could be happy without Romy.

Letting the jumble of feelings overwhelm him. Guilt and grief and resentment for his father. Love and loneliness and joy and despair and desire and everything else that Romy made him feel, everything he had been trying not to feel for so long.

Tears were unmanly. Gerald Gibson had taught his son that long ago, and Lex hadn't cried since he was a very small boy. He didn't cry now, but inside he could feel himself crumbling. He stared straight ahead, his face set like stone, his mouth pressed into a rigid line, and his throat too tight to speak.

To his intense relief, Romy didn't try to make conversation. She just drove him back to the apartment, unlocked the door with the key he handed over without a word, and poured him a great slug of the whisky he had bought for Willie Grant a lifetime ago, all without a word.

Lex sat on the sofa, head bent, the glass clasped between his knees. He swirled the whisky, letting the warm, peaty smell of it calm him before he drank, and its mellowness settled steadyingly in his stomach.

Romy sat quietly beside him, her hand on his back infinitely comforting.

'He never said well done.' The words burst out of him without warning. 'Not once. But do you know what he did? He left me a controlling share in Gibson & Grieve. I had to listen to some lawyer tell me that my father thought I'd done well. That I'd shown I was worthy. He said he was confident that he was leaving the company in capable hands,' said Lex bitterly.

Romy's throat ached for him. 'He was proud of you.'

'It's too late for him to tell me *now*! Why couldn't he…?' He broke off, too angry and frustrated to speak.

'Why couldn't he tell you?' she finished for him. 'Perhaps he was afraid to, Lex. Perhaps, deep down, he was afraid that if he gave you the approval you craved, you wouldn't need him any more.'

She rubbed his back, very gently. 'I think you and I need to forgive our fathers,' she said. 'I certainly need to forgive mine. I loved him so much, but I wanted him to be somebody he couldn't be. I didn't understand that he was just a man, wrestling with his own fears.'

Lex said nothing, but she knew he was listening. 'And your father,' she went on, 'he didn't know how to be a man who could admit weakness. I think he didn't know how to tell you how important you were to him, but that doesn't mean he didn't love you. He just couldn't say it. But he did the best he could, and maybe my father did the best he could, too.'

Lex took a slug of whisky, felt it burn down his throat. 'I thought you would never forgive your father.'

'I thought so, too. It was only when I talked to my mother today, and she made me think. And watching you bury your father, I was imagining how I would feel if it was my father who had died.' Romy swallowed. 'He's the only father I've got. Perhaps I should just accept him for what he is.'

'He hurt you.' Lex looked up at her, pale eyes fierce. 'He left you.'

'He left my mother, not me,' said Romy. 'I think the truth is that *I* left *him* when I refused to see him. I thought that he had chosen his other child over me, but now I think that he chose happiness over duty. Perhaps I need to learn from that. Perhaps we both do.'

'Learn? Learn what?'

'We could learn to be happy,' she said.

'Happy?' Lex stared into his glass and thought of the long, lonely weeks since she'd been gone. The wasteland he had trudged through every day. He thought of the years he had spent trying to forget her, the years he would have to spend forgetting her all over again. '*Happy?* Hah!'

'I thought I could make myself happy,' said Romy as if he hadn't spoken. 'I was afraid to rely on anyone else for happiness. I thought all I needed was to be able to provide for Freya and keep her from being hurt, and I can do that now, but I'm not happy.' She took her hand from his back. 'I can't be happy without you, Lex.'

He did look up at that, his eyes narrowed in sudden attention.

'I don't know if this is the time for it,' she said, 'but there's something I want to ask you.'

'What is it?'

'Will you marry me?'

Lex straightened abruptly, sloshing whisky. *'What?'*

Romy's heart was knocking against her ribs but she made herself look levelly back at him. 'Will you marry me?' she said again. 'I'll understand if you say no,' she said, when he just stared at her. 'I probably deserve it. I had a chance to marry you and I turned it down. We could have had the last twelve years together, but I was too afraid that it would all go wrong.'

Lex put his glass on the table, very carefully, and turned to look at Romy. She was twisting the bangles around her wrist, her eyes huge and dark. 'What's changed? Why aren't you afraid now?'

'I *am* afraid,' she said. 'But I'm more afraid of spending the rest of my life regretting that I was too much of a coward to take a chance at happiness. I'm afraid of spending the rest of my life missing you, the way I've missed you the last few weeks. I'm afraid of never really being happy again without you.'

'Romy…'

'I'm afraid that it might not work,' she said again, 'but I want to take the risk, if you will.'

Lex was looking stunned and Romy took her bottom lip between her teeth, all at once regretting the words that had come tumbling out of her. 'I'm sorry,' she said remorsefully. 'I shouldn't be talking like this, not today. Today should be about your father, not about me. Oh, Lex, I'm sorry,' she said again. 'What was I thinking?'

'Perhaps,' Lex said slowly, 'you were thinking

that this is exactly the day we should be talking like this. Perhaps it takes death to make us realise how we want to live.'

Might it be all right after all? Romy took a breath and let it out very carefully. 'I don't want to live without ever seeing my father again,' she said. 'But most of all, I don't want to live without you, Lex.'

'Romy,' he said again, laying a hand against her cheek. 'Romy, what if I can't make you happy? You're so…*alive*. You need warmth and laughter and love.'

'You love me, don't you?'

He half smiled. 'Yes, I love you. I've never stopped loving you,' he said, unable to stop his fingers slipping under her hair to the nape of her neck. 'Loving you isn't the problem. You were the one who said that. But love wasn't enough before. We're still different people. I'd like to think I can change to be more like you, but what if I can only be like my father?'

'You're not your father,' said Romy, ' and you're not my father either. You're you, and I love you the way you are. You don't have to change. You just have to be brave enough to love me and believe that I love you too, just as I need to be brave enough to trust that you won't leave me and Freya. Love *isn't* enough,' she said. 'We need courage, too, just like Willie said.'

Lex's hand was warm at the nape of her neck. 'Then we'll be brave together,' he said and drew her towards him.

It was a gentle kiss at first, like a first kiss, as if he couldn't quite believe that she was *there*, that she was real. Then it was tender and it was sweet, and the world shifted and righted itself at last.

They kissed and kissed in a torrent of relief, sinking down into the soft cushions until the sweetness grew hard and hungry, but when they broke for breath the world was still right. This, *this*, was right. Romy was lying tucked into him, her arms round him, her face pressed into his throat. Lex could feel her lovely mouth curved into a smile against his skin and the tight band that had been clamped around his chest for so long unlocked and loosened.

He tried breathing in and out experimentally, and the ease of it made his head reel. Wrapping his arms around Romy, he held her close.

'Romy, are you sure?'

'I'm sure,' she said, tilting her head back to kiss his jaw. 'Are you?'

'What about all those practicalities that were such a problem before?'

She wriggled up so that she could look at him properly. 'I suppose we could always take Willie's advice and compromise. Maybe you could learn to live in a less than perfectly ordered flat, and maybe I could learn to tidy up more. I don't think it would be easy, but we could both try.'

'This flat isn't suitable for Freya anyway,' said Lex. 'Why don't we buy a house in Somerset?'

'Somerset's not very convenient for the office,' she pointed out.

'Then we'll have a house in London as well.'

'But you like this flat! It's perfect for you.'

'It wasn't perfect when you left. I hated it without you,' he said. 'I missed you both so much. Every night I'd sit here with the phone in my hand and think about calling you and begging you to come back.'

Romy pulled away slightly, wondering what she would have done if he had called. 'But you never rang?'

'I thought you'd say no. I thought you wanted Freya to get to know her father, and I thought that was the right thing to do. Michael's her father, not me.' Lex hesitated. 'You said it, Romy. You said your father was the only one you'd ever have.'

'But that was me,' she said. 'There was no one else for me. Being a parent is about more than biology,' she told him. 'I hope Michael will always be part of her life, and if he is Freya is going to be lucky. She'll have two fathers, and I hope she'll love you both, but you're the one who's going to teach her to play the piano and comfort her at night when she's teething…oh, and change her nappies, of course!'

Lex laughed at that. 'When you said I had to be brave, I didn't think you meant *that* brave!'

'Losing your nerve?' she asked, smiling, and he pulled her against him for a hard kiss.

'No, I don't mind what I do, as long as I'm with you. I'll even change nappies!'

'Now I know you love me,' said Romy, kissing him back.

'Always,' said Lex.

Pushing herself up so that she could lean over him, Romy rested her hand over his heart. 'You haven't given me an answer yet,' she reminded him. 'I asked you to marry me. Will you?' Stupidly, she could hear a hint of anxiety in her voice.

Lex didn't answer immediately. 'Are you sure you want to be married, Romy?' he asked seriously. 'I know the idea of commitment isn't easy for you. We can be together without marriage if that's more comfortable for you.'

'But that wouldn't be brave,' said Romy. 'I don't want to keep my options open or to know that I can move on if I need to. Lex. I want to spend the rest of my life loving you and trusting you and knowing that every day you'll come home and love me back. Marriage is a promise. I want to make that promise in front of everybody, and I want to keep it, with you.'

Lex picked up the hand that covered his heart and kissed her palm before he drew her down to him once more. 'Then since you ask so nicely,' he said, 'yes, I will.'